Dick King-Smith's
Countryside Treasury

Illustrated by Christian Birmingham

Collins
An Imprint of HarperCollinsPublishers

To Thomas and Zöe
CB

First published in Great Britain by HarperCollins Publishers Ltd in 1998

1 3 5 7 9 10 8 6 4 2
ISBN: 0 00 198161-7

Introduction and compilation copyright © Fox Busters Ltd 1998
Illustration copyright © Christian Birmingham 1998
The compiler and illustrator assert the moral right to be identified as the compiler and
illustrator of the work.
A CIP catalogue record for this title is available from the British Library.

Printed and bound in Singapore by Imago

CONTENTS

INTRODUCTION   4

CHILDHOOD   5

ANIMALS   37

COUNTRY WAYS   87

ARCADIA   115

INDEX OF TITLES AND FIRST LINES   140

INDEX OF AUTHORS   143

ACKNOWLEDGEMENTS   144

INTRODUCTION

I think that I'm fortunate to have always lived in the same little bit of country. "He lives," it says inside many of my books, "in a 17th century cottage a short crow's-flight from the house where he was born." (Ever since, I have been on the lookout for a short crow).

This is not to belittle all sorts of other areas in which it would be pleasant to have one's home, but rather to sing the praises of my patch.

To the north of me lie the Cotswolds, to the south the Mendips, to the West is the Bristol Channel and Wales beyond it, to the East the Wiltshire Downs. I am lucky enough, in fact, to be surrounded by differing types of countryside, of which there are so many in these islands.

We have highlands and lowlands and uplands called downlands, and woodlands and lakelands and moorlands and marshlands, all supporting a wonderful mix of animals and plants. It's small wonder that so many writers have used our countryside as a backcloth for their stories, and so many poets as a frame for their word-pictures. We are all lucky, in my opinion, to be able to enjoy the four seasons, each with its particular attractions in a temperate climate where we don't, generally speaking, have to endure extremes of heat or cold or drought or flood, and can be fairly confident that hurricanes hardly ever happen and that earthquakes are rather rare and pretty puny.

As to my choices for this anthology, I'm on a hiding to nothing, I know. "Why did he leave that out?" people will say of a favourite piece. "Why ever didn't he put this in?"

The answer quite simply lies in an *embarras des richesses*. So many wonderful words have been written about our countryside that, had I been let off the leash, we'd have ended up with a book far too heavy to lift.

I just hope that, in this selection, there'll be something for everyone.

Dick King-Smith

CHILDHOOD

Where the pools are bright and deep,
Where the grey trout lies asleep,
Up the river and o'er the lea –
That's the way for Billy and me.

Where the blackbird sings the latest,
Where the hawthorn blooms the sweetest,
Where the nestlings chirp and flee –
That's the way for Billy and me.

from THE PEPPERMINT PIG

She came out of the scullery, drying her hands and muttering under her breath. She forgot to pick up the blue and white jug from the table and when she reached the door, she called Poll to bring it.

The milkman was saying, "...so the old sow farrowed early. D'you want a peppermint pig, Mrs Greengrass?"

Poll looked at him, thinking of sweets, but there was a real pig poking its snout out of the milkman's coat pocket. It was the tiniest pig she had ever seen. She touched its hard little head and said, "What's a peppermint pig?"

"Not worth much," Mother said. "Only a token. Like a peppercorn rent. Almost nothing."

"Runt of the litter," the milkman added. "Too small for the sow to raise. He'd only get trampled in the rush."

Mother took the pig from him and held it firmly while it kicked and squealed piercingly. She tipped it to look at its stomach and said, "Well, he seems strong enough. And even runts grow."

The milkman took the jug from Poll and went to his cart to ladle milk out of his churn.

"Oh," Poll said. "Oh, *Mother*." She stroked the small, wriggling body. Stroked one way, its skin felt silky to touch; the other way, stiff little hairs prickled her fingers. He was a pale apricot colour all over.

The milkman came back. Mother said, "Will you take a shilling?" and he nodded and grinned. Poll took the milk to the kitchen and flew upstairs for her mother's purse. "Theo," she shouted, "look what we've got!"

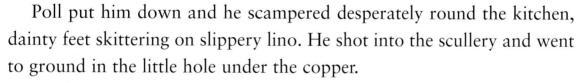

An old pint beer mug stood on the dresser. Mother laughed suddenly and popped the pig in it. He made such a fearsome noise that they put their hands over their ears. Poll picked him out and said, "Whatever made you do that?"

"I just thought he would fit, and he did!"

Poll put him down and he scampered desperately round the kitchen, dainty feet skittering on slippery lino. He shot into the scullery and went to ground in the little hole under the copper.

Mother said, "Leave him now, poor little fellow, he's scared to death. He'll settle down while you're at school."

Poll groaned tragically. "Must we go? Oh, I can't bear it, I can't bear to leave him."

"He'll be here when you come home dinner time," Mother said.

Poll counted the hours. Not just that day, but the next and the next, the thought of the baby pig, waiting at home, distracted her attention so she had no time left to be naughty: by the end of the first week, she had not once been rapped over the knuckles or stood in the corner. She made a best friend called Annie Dowsett who was older than she was and who told her how babies were born. "The butcher comes and cuts you up the stomach with his carving knife," Annie said. "But don't tell your mother I told you." Poll didn't really believe this, because if it were true, women would never have more than one baby, but it was an interesting idea all the same and she began to feel she quite liked this new school. She even liked her teacher, Miss Armstrong, who had a long, mild, sheep's face, and was proud that her Aunt was Headmistress with her name on a brass plate on the outside of the building. Everyone was a little scared of Aunt Sarah but not of Aunt Harriet who was called, Miss Harry to her face and Old Harry behind her back, who romped in the playground with the little ones until her wispy hair came down under her hat, and always brought potatoes to school to bake in the stove for the children who lived too far away to go home for their dinner.

Even Theo was happier because of the pig. The excitement of its arrival carried him through the first day, and although after that the horrible shame of the pink, girlish vest hidden under his clothes still haunted him sleeping and walking, especially when he caught Noah Bugg's rolling, gooseberry eye in the classroom, he managed to live with it. No one, he told himself, was likely to fall upon him and tear his clothes off, and even if he was sometimes tormented because of his size, he was used to that, and it was a comfort to run home and pick up the pig and whisper in his floppy ear, "Peppermint pig, peppermint pig, I'm a peppermint *boy*, so there's two of us, runts in this family."

Mother called the pig Johnnie, saying (rather oddly the children thought) that he reminded her of her grandfather, and it wasn't long before he answered to his name, grunting and running whenever they called him. At night, he slept in the copper hole on a straw bed; during the day he trotted busily round behind Mother or sat on the hearth rug staring thoughtfully into the fire.

Lily said, "You can't keep a pig indoors, Mother!"

"Oh, we had all sorts of animals in the house when I was young," Mother said. "Jackdaws, hedgehogs, newly hatched chicks. I remember times you couldn't get near our fire."

"But not *pig*s," Lily said.

"I can't see why not. You'd keep a dog and a pig has more brains than

9

a dog let me tell you. If you mean pigs are dirty, that's just a matter of giving a pig a bad name to my mind. Why, our Johnnie was house-trained in a matter of days and with a good deal less trouble than *you* gave me, my girl!"

Poll giggled and Lily went pink.

Mother said, "Give a pig a chance to keep clean and he'll take it, which is more than you can say of some humans. You tell me now, does Johnnie smell?"

If he did, it was only of a mixture of bran and sweet milk which was all he ate to begin with, although as he grew older, Mother boiled up small potatoes and added scraps from the table. She said there was no waste in a house with a pig and when the summer came they would go round the hedgerows and collect dandelions and sow thistle so he would have plenty of fresh food and grow strong and healthy. "What he eats is important," she said. "Pigs are a poor person's investment."

Nina Bawden

from THE COUNTRY CHILD

Mornings began with mists like pools of milk upset in the valleys, into which Susan ran helter-skelter to school. Gossamer, beaded with jewels, bound together the bracken and heather, the trees and ferns. The briars, the hedgerows, the bushes were covered with millions of tiny webs, beaded like fair necklaces with dewdrops. Her feet broke silvery meshes spread like a net over the wet grass, and she left dark footprints as if she walked in snow. Soon the first hoar-frost would come, powdering the world, making a wood a vast jeweller's shop in the morning, a haunted palace at night.

Down the lane the briar hung in circles and garlands with ruddy-veined leaves and cursed ill-luck late blackberries. Susan picked up fallen acorns and gathered bunches of nuts as she skipped through the wood, families of five and six on a stem, which she took to school.

She snatched branches of hawthorn and ate the fleshy crimson aiges as her breakfast dessert, washing them down with water from a spring which ran through the bracken.

Alison Uttley

from KILVERT'S DIARY 1870-1879

Saturday, 16 January

In the Common Field in front of the cottages I found two little figures in the dusk. One tiny urchin was carefully binding a handkerchief round the face of an urchin even more tiny than himself. It was Fred and Jerry Savine. "What are you doing to him?" I asked Fred. "Please, Sir," said the child solemnly. "Please, Sir, we'm gwine to play at blindman's buff." The two children were quite alone. The strip of dusky meadow was like a marsh and every footstep trod the water out of the soaked land, but the two little images went solemnly on with their game as if they were in a magnificent playground with a hundred children to play with. Oh, the wealth of a child's imagination and capacity for enjoyment of trifles.

The Reverend Francis Kilvert

from TALES OF ARABEL'S RAVEN

Arabel was little and fair with grey eyes. She was wearing a white nightdress that made her look like a lampshade with two feet sticking out from the bottom. One of the feet had a blue sock on.

"What's the matter, Ma?" she said.

"There's a great awful *bird* in the fridge!" sobbed Mrs Jones. "And it's eaten all the cheese and a blackcurrant tart and five pints of milk and a bowl of dripping and a pound of sausages. All that's left is the lettuce."

"Then we'll have lettuce for breakfast," said Arabel.

But Mrs Jones said she didn't fancy lettuce that had spent the night in the fridge with a great awful bird. "And how are we going to get it out of there?"

"The lettuce?"

"The *bird*!" said Mrs Jones, switching off the kettle and pouring hot water into a pot without any tea in it.

Arabel opened the fridge door, which had swung shut. There sat the bird, among the empty milk bottles, but he was a lot bigger than they were. There was a certain amount of wreckage around him – torn foil, and cheese wrappings, and milk splashes, and bits of pastry, and crumbs of dripping, and rejected lettuce leaves. It was like Rumbury Waste after a picnic Sunday.

Arabel looked at the raven, and he looked back at her.

"His name's Mortimer," she said.

"No it's not, no it's not!" cried Mrs Jones, taking a loaf from the bread bin and absent-mindedly running the tap over it. "We said you could have a hamster when you were five, or a puppy or a kitten when you were six, and of course call it what you wish, oh my *stars*, look at that creature's toe-nails, if nails they can be called, but not a bird like that, a great hairy awful thing eating us out of house and home, as big as a fire extinguisher and all black –" But Arabel was looking at the raven and he was looking back at her. "His name's Mortimer," she said. And she put both arms round the raven, not an easy thing to do, all jammed in among the milk bottles as he was, and lifted him out.

"He's very heavy," she said, and set him down on the kitchen floor.

"So I should think, considering he's got a pound of sausages, a bowl of dripping, five pints of milk, half a pound of New Zealand cheddar, and a blackcurrant tart inside him," said Mrs Jones. "I'll open the window. Perhaps he'll fly out."

She opened the window. But Mortimer did not fly out. He was busy examining everything in the kitchen very thoroughly. He tapped the table legs with his beak – they were metal, and clinked. Then he took everything out of the waste bin – a pound of peanut shells, two empty tins, and some jam tart cases. He particularly liked the jam tart cases, which he pushed under the lino. Then he walked over to the fireplace – it was an old-fashioned kitchen – and began chipping out the mortar from between the bricks.

Mrs Jones had been gazing at the raven as if she were under a spell, but when he began on the fireplace, she said, "*Don't* let him do that."

"Mortimer," said Arabel, "we'd like you not to do that, please."

Mortimer turned his head right round on its black feathery neck and gave Arabel a thoughtful, considering look. Then he made his first remark, which was a deep, hoarse, rasping croak.

Joan Aiken

WHITE FIELDS

In winter-time we go
Walking in the fields of snow;

Where there is no grass at all;
Where the top of every wall,

Every fence and every tree,
Is as white as white can be.

Pointing out the way we came –
Every one of them the same –

All across the fields there be
Prints in silver filigree:

And our mothers always know
By the footprints in the snow,

Where it is the children go.

James Stephens

from THE POACHER'S SON

When Arthur's dad loses his job as underkeeper on a large estate, his family have to move away to a remote cottage. Arthur frequently truants from school to explore Pit Bottom wood behind their new home.

As I entered the wood, I broke through a new web spun between two bushes. It was so fine I could not see it and it was only as I felt the invisible stickiness stroke against my cheeks and saw the blowflies dangling in mid-air, that I realized I had destroyed the spider's food source. I climbed a young oak on the edge of the wood, settled myself comfortably into the curved arm of the tree to listen, to watch, and to become part of the life of the wood. A wood-pigeon, startled by my arrival, settled down again on the branch immediately above to preen. So long as I stayed still, there was little chance that he would see me. A pigeon, once perched, rarely looks straight down.

From that height, I could see right across the fields as far as the village, where the low blueish shapes of the dwellings and the church and the school stood out against the brown and green of the fields.

I wondered if perhaps Humphrey was standing in for me, to call out for me when the register was taken. He had done so before now, answering to both his name and mine so that my absences – as recorded in the black book – did not seem quite as many as really they were. With nearly forty children in his care, from little 'uns of barely five years, up to big boys of going on fourteen, Mr Pooley was often confused.

Humphrey was three years younger than me, but I was small for my age and we both had the same bright hair and red cheeks. Many people took us for the same person, so long as they didn't see us together.

I looked away from the village and back up into the wood. Already Humphrey could read and write better than I could. He had passed his Standard 3 last year. Perhaps he would end up with brains as good as Alice, and then, like her, he might become a teacher. If that happened, I should certainly be proud of him, but it wouldn't make me envy him.

With my catapult, I shot a crow for sport. I picked up the corpse and fastened it to a fence, alongside six dead weasels whose shrivelled skins flapped in the breeze like grey washing.

I watched a kestrel hover, sizing up a creature in the rough grass below. It plummeted like a dropped stone, caught nothing and within moments, was up again, quivering in the same spot, as though that piece of sky was visibly marked. It waited and swooped four times before it finally caught its prey and made off to the privacy of the woods.

All day, sounds of school drifted up from the village. At intervals, I heard the shouts of children released into the yard, the slam of a door, a distant wavering of a handbell, then silence. At school, children had to do everything by the bell, whether or not they were ready. Here, time did not rule my day. When I was hungry, I dropped down from the tree, like the kestrel to the ground, and found a place to eat. Our dokey on schooldays was always the same. Two pieces of bread spread thickly with dripping. It tasted rich and salty and, though not as filling as a proper hot meal, the pork taste reminded you of the supper you had had the night before, and more important of the hot meal you were going to get in the evening.

The poor prisoners in school had to eat their dokey sitting at their desks. I ate mine in the comfort of an old hayrick. If they were thirsty, they had to ask permission to go out to the pump.

I lay down on the grass and drank from the stream. I trailed my hands amongst the weeds, I tried to catch water-snails on a blade of grass. I smelled the sweet smell of crushed watercress that grew all along the bank.

I didn't like its sharp mustardy taste, but Ma and Pa did, so I gathered a big armful to give to them. Then I remembered, and threw it back into the stream and watched it drift away downstream like a green swan's nest. To take it back would show where I had spent the day.

It had been a good day, as were all days spent in the woods. I was cheerful and confident as I made my way back across the fields to meet up with Alice and Humphrey on their way home from school.

Rachel Anderson

BEING GYPSY

A gypsy, a gypsy,
Is what I'd like to be,
If ever I could find one who
Would change his place with me.

Rings on my fingers,
Earrings in my ears,
Rough shoes to roam the world
For years and years and years!

I'd listen to the stars,
I'd listen to the dawn,
I'd learn the tunes of wind and rain,
The talk of fox and faun.

A gypsy, a gypsy!
To ramble and to roam
For maybe – oh,
A week or so –
And then I'd hie me home!

Barbara Young

from THE LONE SWALLOWS

Henry Williamson, author of 'Tarka the Otter', loved to watch from his Devon cottage the swallows and martins in the nearby brook collecting mud for their homes.

Sometimes a little boy comes and stands by me, and watches them too. He is a funny little fellow, about two and a half years old, with yellow curls and solemn brown eyes. His name is Ernie, and his father is a labourer, a very kind man. He used to spend all his money in the inn, but suddenly took a wife, and drank no more. When Ernie is a naughty boy, he threatens to go "up to pub," and Ernie wails immediately, and is good again.

"I got this one," says Ernie, coming to the cottage door, and holding out in filthy paw a piece of cake. "You ain't got this one, 'ave ee?"

"Go away, Ernie, I'm writing."

"You ain't got this one," he replies, munching the cake, "'ave ee, Mis'r Wisson?"

I feel more comfortable in the company of children than with "grown-ups"; and to discourage his talk I put my tongue out, and make a hideous face.

"Ah'll cut ees tongue off, ah wull," he gravely warns, repeating what his mother has said to him when he has done it to her – a frequent happening, I fear; I taught him to do it.

"Good-bye," I shout.

Then he departs, and five minutes later I hear a feeble "'onk-'onk-'onk" in my garden. Ernie is driving his car, which he had made from my wheelbarrow, a cinder sifter, and an egg-shaped pair of pram-wheels.

"'Onk-'onk," he cries to the sparrows, "git out, 'onk-'onk." Then on seeing me: "I got this one. You ain't got this one, 'ave ee?"

"Noomye!" I exclaim, while Ernie goes faster and faster.

This motor-car is not the only toy. The pram-wheels, or "wills," as he calls them, are a source of happiness. A broom tied to the axle acts as a horse, and Ernie goes driving in the road. Other small brats come up, and a puppy dog or two, and great fun they have, often ending up in the stream.

Ernie's mother is always finding him in the water. She cannot keep him away. He goes out in a clean jersey, knickers, and socks, and suddenly there is a cry for Ernie, a rushing past the door, a curse from myself, and a loud wail.

"You come out of that water, my boy! I told you not to go in that water. Little devil, you," cries the exasperated mother.

"Ah'll tull feyther," shrieks Ernie, as he is driven past the door. His sobs grow less, and a minute later he comes back and stares at me.

"I got some good water," he informs me. "You ain't got no water, 'ave ee?" And he toddles away for more.

He delights in the filthiest old can or bottle. He loves to kneel down and see the water bubbling in. Sometimes it is a "cup of tea" he has got, or a "glass of beer." And always he has "got this one."

Henry Williamson

from STILL GLIDES THE STREAM

But here, at the church stile, she felt at home once more. The little grey church was unaltered, every stone, tile, and weather-worn carving, were exactly as she remembered. The flagstones of the pathway had become mossed at the edges as if fewer feet trod them than formerly, but the yews looked not a day older, and the chestnut by the stile beneath which she was standing was no more widely spreading. The wood pigeons, descendants many times removed from those she had mocked in her childhood, "Take two cows, Taffy! Take two cows, Taffy!" kept up the same perpetual moaning. Even the stile upon which she was leaning had not altered. It was still the same substantial structure, with high mounting-stools and a rounded beam for a top rail. "'T'ould take a charge of dynamite to shift this," her father had once said as he crossed it, and he had spoken authoritatively as a craftsman. The rounded top rail had been polished to glassiness by the Sunday trouser-seats of generations of village youths whose favourite perch it had been while waiting for the chimes to stop and the little *ting-tang* bell to tell them that the parson was getting into his surplice, when they would shuffle in a body up the flagstone path and tip-toe into the seat nearest the door, determined not to spend indoors a moment more than was necessary.

Flora Thompson

from CHANGE IN THE VILLAGE

George Bourne was a critic of the enclosure of common land of the late 18th/19thC, which he believed had caused social damage. In 'Change in the Village', he presented a nostalgic vision of village life before enclosure.

"Matter-of-fact" is what the children are, for the most part. One autumn evening, after dark, tittering and little squeals of excitement sounded from a neighbour's garden, where a man, going to draw water from his well, and carrying a lantern, was accompanied by four or five children. In the security of his presence they were pretending to be afraid of "bogies". "If a bogie was to come," I heard, "I should get up that apple-tree, and

then if he come up after me I should get down t'other side." An excited laugh was followed by the man's contemptuous remonstrance, "*Shut up!*" which produced silence for a minute or two, until the party were returning to the cottage; when a very endearing voice called softly, "Bo-gie! Bo-gie! Come, bogie!" This instance of fancy in a cottage child stands, however, alone in my experience. I have never heard anything else like it in the village. The children romp and squabble and make much noise; they play, though rarely, at hide-and-seek; or else they gambol about aimlessly, or try to sing together, or troop off to look at the fowls or the rabbits. The bigger children are as a rule extremely kind to the lesser ones. A family of small brothers and sisters who lived near me some time ago were most pleasant to listen to for this reason. The smallest of them, a three-year-old boy commonly called "'Arry", was their pet. "Look, 'Arry; here's a *dear* little flow-wer! A little 'arts-ease – look, 'Arry!" "'Ere, 'Arry, have a bite o' this nice apple!" They were certainly attractive children, though formidably grubby as to their faces. I heard them with their father, admiring a litter of young rabbits in the hutch. "O-oh, en't that a *dear* little thing!" they exclaimed, again and again. Sunday was especially delightful to them because their father was at home then; and I liked to hear him playing with them. One particularly happy hour they had, in which he feigned to be angry and they to be defiant. They jumped about just out of his reach, jeering at him. "Old Father Smither!" they cried, as often as their peals of laughter would let them cry anything at all.

George Bourne

from THE VIEW IN WINTER

Ronald Blythe remembers how he used to go fishing with his friends when he was a boy. They would catch eels, and skin them and then take them home to boil and fry them. But none of the boys liked to eat pike.

But father loved a pike. So I'd snare him one with a leather bootlace. I'd see a pike lay in the river and I'd take this long ol' leather lace and make it into a loop. Then I'd hang it from a pole and gradually, *gradually*, hold me breath, I'd lower it down right in front of him, this still, still pike. Inter the slip-knot he'd goo and out on the bank he'd come! I caught hundreds o' pike like that – hundreds! They'd be that riled!

Ronald Blythe

from HIAWATHA'S CHILDHOOD

And the good Nokomis answered:
"That is but the owl and owlet,
Talking in their native language,
Talking, scolding at each other."
   Then the little Hiawatha
Learned of every bird its language,
Learned their names and all their secrets,
How they built their nests in Summer,
Where they hid themselves in Winter,
Talked with them whene'er he met them,
Called them "Hiawatha's Chickens."
   Of all beasts he learned the language,
Learned their names and all their secrets,
How the beavers built their lodges,
Where the squirrels hid their acorns,
How the reindeer ran so swiftly,
Why the rabbit was so timid,
Talked with them whene'er he met them,
Called them "Hiawatha's Brothers."

Henry Wadsworth Longfellow

from JUDE THE OBSCURE

The boy stood under the rick before mentioned, and every few seconds used his clacker or rattle briskly. At each clack the rooks left off pecking, and rose and went away on their leisurely wings, burnished like tassets of mail, afterwards wheeling back and regarding him warily, and descending to feed at a more respectful distance.

He sounded the clacker till his arm ached, and at length his heart grew sympathetic with the birds' thwarted desires. They seemed, like himself, to be living in a world which did not want them. Why should he frighten them away? They took upon them more and more the aspect of gentle friends and pensioners – the only friends he could claim as being in the least degree interested in him, for his aunt had often told him that she was not. He ceased his rattling, and they alighted anew.

"Poor little dears!" said Jude, aloud. "You *shall* have some dinner – you shall. There is enough for us all. Farmer Troutham can afford to let you have some. Eat, then, my dear little birdies, and make a good meal!"

29

They stayed and ate, inky spots on the nut-brown soil, and Jude enjoyed their appetite. A magic thread of fellow-feeling united his own life with theirs. Puny and sorry as those lives were, they much resembled his own.

His clacker he had by this time thrown away from him, as being a mean and sordid instrument, offensive both to the birds and to himself as their friend. All at once he became conscious of a smart blow upon his buttock, followed by a loud clack, which announced to his surprised senses that the clacker had been the instrument of offence used. The birds and Jude started up simultaneously, and the dazed eyes of the latter beheld the farmer in person, the great Troutham himself, his red face glaring down upon Jude's cowering frame, the clacker swinging in his hand.

"So it's 'Eat, my dear birdies,' is it, young man? 'Eat, dear birdies,' indeed! I'll tickle your breeches, and see if you say, 'Eat, dear birdies,' again in a hurry! And you've been idling at the schoolmaster's too, instead of coming here, ha'n't ye, hey? That's how you earn your sixpence a day for keeping the rooks off my corn!"

Whilst saluting Jude's ears with his impassioned rhetoric, Troutham had seized his left hand with his own left, and swinging his slim frame round him at arm's-length, again struck Jude on the hind parts with the flat side of Jude's own rattle, till the field echoed with the blows, which were delivered once or twice at each revolution.

"Don't 'ee, sir – please don't 'ee!" cried the whirling child, as helpless under the centrifugal tendency of his person as a hooked fish swinging to land, and beholding the hill, the rick, the plantation, the path and the rooks going round and round him in an amazing circular race. "I – I – sir – only meant that – there was a good crop in the ground – I saw 'em sow it – and the rooks could have a little bit for dinner – and you wouldn't miss it, sir – and Mr Phillotson said I was to be kind to 'em – O, O, O!"

Thomas Hardy

from THE WHISTLER AT THE PLOUGH

This conversation with a ploughboy was part of a survey of farm life undertaken in 1852 by agricultural reformers.

"You hold the plough, you say; how old are you?"

"I bees sixteen a'most."

"What wages have you?"

"Three shillin' a-week."

"Three shillings! Have you nothing else? Don't you get victuals, or part of them, from your master?"

"No, I buys them all."

"All out of three shillings?"

"Ees, and buys my clothes out of that."

"And what do you buy to eat?"

"Buy to eat! Why, I buys bread and lard."

"Do you eat bread and lard always? What have you for breakfast?"

"What have I for breakfast? Why, bread and lard."

"And what for dinner?"

"Bread and lard."

"What for supper, the same?"

"Ees, the same for supper – bread and lard."

"It seems to be always bread and lard, have you no boiled bacon and vegetables?"

"No, there be no place to boil 'em; no time to boil 'em; none to boil."

"Have you never a hot dinner nor supper; don't you get potatoes?"

"Ees, potatoes, an we pay for 'em. Master lets us boil 'em once a-week an we like."

"And what do you eat to them; bacon?"

"No."

"What then?"

"Lard; never has nothing but lard."

"Can't you boil potatoes or cook your victuals any day you choose?"

"No; has no fire."

"Have you no fire to warm you in cold weather?"

"No, we never has fire."

"Where do you go in the winter evenings?"

"To bed, when it be time; an it ben't time, we goes to some of the housen as be round about."

"To the firesides of some of the cottagers, I suppose?"

"Ees, an we can get."

"What if you cannot get; do you go into the farm-house?"

"No, mustn't; never goes nowhere but to bed an it be very cold."

"Where is your bed?"

"In the *tollit*" (stable loft).

"How many of you sleep there?"

"All on us as be hired."

"How many are hired?"

"Four last year, five this."

" Does any one make your beds for you?"

"No, we make 'em ourselves."

"Who washes your sheets?"

"Who washes 'em?"

"Yes; they *are* washed, I suppose?"

"No, they ben't."

"What! never washed? Do you mean to say you don't have your sheets washed?"

"No, never since I comed."

"When did you come?"

"Last Michaelmas."

"Were your bedclothes clean then?"

"I dare say they was."

"And don't you know how long they are to serve until they are changed again?"

"To Michaelmas, I hear tell."

"So one change of bedclothes serves a year! Don't you find your bed disagreeable?"

"Do I! I bees too sleepy. I never knows nought of it, only that I has to get up afore I be awake, and never get into it afore I be a'most asleep. I be up at four, and ben't done work afore eight at night."

"You don't go so long at the plough as that?"

"No; but master be always having summat for we to do as be hired; we be always at summat."

Alexander Somerville

HEDGES

"Bread and cheese" grow wild in the green time,
Children laugh and pick it, and I make my rhyme
For mere pleasure of seeing that so subtle play
Of arms and various legs going every, any way.

And they turn and laugh for the unexpensiveness
Of country grocery and are pleased no less
Than hedge sparrows. Lessons will be easier taken,
For this gipsy chaffering, the hedge plucked and shaken.

Ivor Gurney

I Will Go with my Father a-Ploughing

I will go with my Father a-ploughing
To the Green Field by the sea,
And the rooks and crows and seagulls
Will come flocking after me.
I will sing to the patient horses
With the lark in the shine of the air,
And my Father will sing the Plough-Song
That blesses the cleaving share.

I will go with my Father a-sowing
To the Red Field by the sea,
And blackbirds and robins and thrushes
Will come flocking after me.
I will sing to the striding sowers
With the finch on the flowering sloe,
And my Father will sing the Seed-Song
That only the wise men know.

I will go with my Father a-reaping
To the Brown Field by the sea,
And the geese and pigeons and sparrows
Will come flocking after me.
I will sing to the weary reapers
With the wren in the heat of the sun,
And my Father will sing the Scythe-Song
That joys for the harvest done.

Joseph Campbell

ANIMALS

The robin sings in the elm;
The cattle stand beneath,
Sedate and grave with great brown eyes,
And fragrant meadow-breath.

They listen to the flattered bird,
The wise-looking, stupid things!
And they never understand a word
Of all the robin sings.

from THE SHEEP-PIG

"Oh hullo, young un," puffed the old sheep. "Fine day you chose to come, I'll say."

"What is it? What's happening? Who are these men?" asked Babe.

"Rustlers," said Ma. "They'm sheep-rustlers."

"What d'you mean?"

"Thieves, young un, that's what I do mean. Sheep-stealers. We'll all be in thik lorry afore you can blink your eye."

"What can we do?"

"Do? Ain't nothing we can do, unless we can slip past theseyer wolf."

She made as if to escape, but the dog behind darted in, and she turned back.

Again, one of the men whistled, and the dog pressed. Gradually, held against the headland of the field by the second dog and the men, the flock began to move forward. Already the leaders were nearing the tailboard of the lorry.

"We'm beat," said Ma mournfully. "You run for it, young un." I will, thought Babe, but not the way you mean. Little as he was, he felt suddenly not fear but anger, furious anger that the boss's sheep were being stolen. My mum's not here to protect them so I must, he said to himself bravely, and he ran quickly round the hedge side of the flock, and jumping on to the bottom of the tailboard, turned to face them.

"Please!" he cried. "I beg you! Please don't come any further. If you would be so kind, dear, sensible sheep!"

His unexpected appearance had a number of immediate effects. The shock of being so politely addressed stopped the flock in its tracks, and the cries of "Wolf!" changed to murmurs of "In't he lovely!" and "Proper little gennulman!" Ma had told them something of her new friend, and now to see him in the flesh and to hear his well-chosen words released them from the dominance of the dogs. They began to fidget and look about for an escape route. This was opened for them when the men (cursing quietly, for above all things they were anxious to avoid too much noise) sent the flanking dog to drive the pig away, and some of the sheep began to slip past them.

Next moment all was chaos. Angrily the dog ran at Babe, who scuttled away squealing at the top of his voice in a mixture of fright and fury. The men closed on him, sticks raised. Desperately he shot between the legs of one, who fell with a crash, while the other, striking out madly, hit the rearguard dog as it came to help, and sent it howling. In half a minute the carefully planned raid was ruined, as the sheep scattered everywhere.

"Keep yelling, young un!" bawled Ma, as she ran beside Babe. "They won't never stop here with that row going on!"

And suddenly all sorts of things began to happen as those deafening squeals rang out over the quiet countryside. Birds flew startled from the trees, cows in nearby fields began to gallop about, dogs in distant farms to bark, passing motorists to stop and stare. In the farmhouse below, Mrs Hogget heard the noise as she had on the day of the Fair, but now it was infinitely louder, the most piercing, nerve-tingling, ear-shattering burglar alarm. She dialled 999 but then talked for so long that by the time a patrol car drove up the lane, the rustlers had long gone. Snarling at each other and their dogs, they had driven hurriedly away with not one single sheep to show for their pains.

"You won't never believe it!" cried Mrs Hogget when her husband returned from the market. "But we've had rustlers, just after you'd gone it were, come with a girt cattle-lorry they did, the police said, they seen the tyremarks in the gateway, and a chap in a car seen the lorry go by in a hurry, and there's been a lot of it about, and he give the alarm, he did, kept screaming and shrieking enough to bust your eardrums, we should have lost every sheep on the place if 'tweren't for him, 'tis him we've got to thank."

"Who?" said Farmer Hogget.

"Him!" said his wife, pointing at Babe who was telling Fly all about it. "Don't ask me how he got there or why he done it, all I knows is he saved our bacon and now I'm going to save his, he's stopping with us just like another dog, don't care if he gets so big as a house, because if you think I'm going to stand by and see him butchered after what he done for us today, you've got another think coming, what d'you say to that?"

A slow smile spread over Farmer Hogget's long face.

Dick King-Smith

MINNOWS

Swarms of minnows show their little heads,
Staying their wavy bodies 'gainst the streams,
To taste the luxury of sunny beams
Tempered with coolness. How they ever wrestle
With their own sweet delight, and ever nestle
Their silver bellies on the pebbly sand.
If you but scantily hold out the hand,
That very instant not one will remain;
But turn your eye, and they are there again.
The ripples seem right glad to reach those cresses,
And cool themselves among the em'rald tresses;
The while they cool themselves, they freshness give,
And moisture, that the bowery green may live.

John Keats

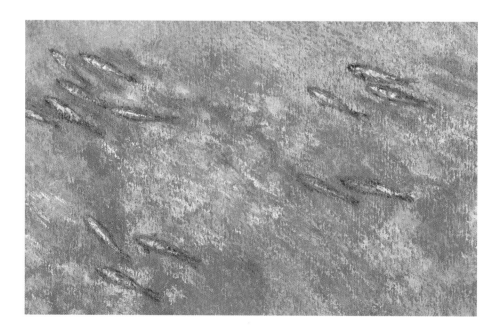

THE CUCKOO

The cuckoo is a merry bird,
   He sings as he flies,
He brings us glad tidings,
   And tells us no lies.

He sucks the birds' eggs
   To make his voice clear,
And the more he cries "Cuckoo!"
   The summer draws near.

The cuckoo is a lazy bird,
   She never builds a nest,
She makes herself busy
   By singing to the rest;

She never hatches her own young,
   And that we all know,
But leaves it for some other bird
   While she cries "Cuckoo!"

And when her time is come
   Her voice we no longer hear,
And where she goes we do not know
   Until another year.

The cuckoo comes in April,
   She sings a song in May,
In June she beats upon the drum, *
   And then she'll fly away.

Anon

* *The cuckoo is said to "beat the drum" when he often falters and cries "Cuck-cuck-cuck," without the final syllable. This is said to be a sign of his impending departure.*

from SALAR THE SALMON

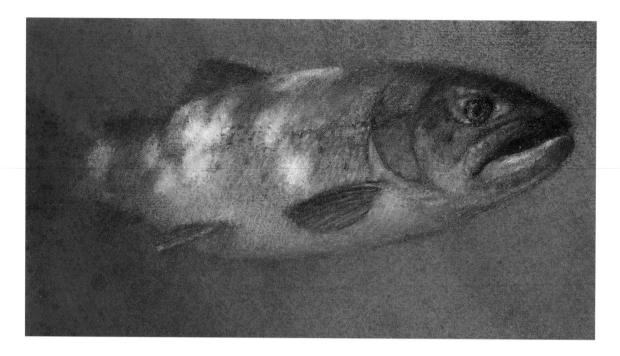

Salar had avoided death by bite of porpoise, shark, ray, and other predatory fish – nearly all fish prey on other fish – and now, five years and one month since hatching from a round egg about three-sixteenths of an inch in diameter in the head-waters of a stream under Snowdon, he was more than a yard long, and his girth was half his length.

He was lying on the edge of a current where it dragged against an eddy or back-trend of water; using one moving weight of water to buoy him against an opposing weight. He lolled there, at rest. He was nearly asleep. His mouth opened to take in water twenty times a minute.

Two lines of pierced scales along each flank covered cells filled with liquid which was sensitive to every varying pressure of moving water; the cells were joined with nerve-roots which connected with the brain. His body moved in idle flexion. Fins kept the body poised in its hover. On his back was the dorsal fin, behind each gill-cover was a pectoral fin. A little behind the point of the body's balance were the paired or ventral fins, by which he held himself when resting on a rock, or the bed of the sea in

44

shallow water. By the caudal or tail fin he steered himself: a rudder. There was a small fixed fin, like a pennon, on his back, aft of the dorsal fin, which served to prevent turbulence or eddy when he was swimming forward. Blue and silver of flanks, porcelain white of belly, with fins of a delicate opaque greyish-pink, with a few yellow-red and grey-green and light brown spots on his gill-covers, and groups of sea-lice under the dark edge of his tail and on his back, Salar was resting in one of the many streaming currents at the eastern edge of the Island Race when Jarrk swam down, driving himself by powerful flippers, peering round and below with grey-filmy eyes.

Henry Williamson

HOW THE HARE BECAME

Now Hare was a real dandy. He was about the vainest creature on the whole earth.

Every morning he spent one hour smartening his fur, another hour smoothing his whiskers, and another cleaning his paws. Then the rest of the day he strutted up and down, admiring his shadow, and saying:

"How handsome I am! How amazingly handsome! Surely some great princess will want to marry me soon."

The other creatures grew so tired of his vain ways that they decided to teach him a lesson. Now they knew that he would believe any story so long as it made him think he was handsome. So this is what they did:

One morning Gazelle went up to Hare and said:

"Good morning, Hare. How handsome you look. No wonder we've been hearing such stories about you."

"Stories?" asked Hare. "What stories?"

"Haven't you heard the news?" cried Gazelle. "It's about you."

"News? News? What news?" cried Hare, jumping up and down in excitement.

"Why, the moon wants to marry you," said Gazelle. "The beautiful moon, the queen of the night sky. She wants to marry you because she says you're the handsomest creature in the whole world. Oh yes. You should just have heard a few of the things she was saying about you last night."

"Such as?" cried Hare. "Such as?" He could hardly wait to hear what fine things moon had said about him.

"Never mind now," said Gazelle. "But she'll be walking up that hill tonight; and if you want to marry her, you're to be there to meet her. Lucky man!"

Gazelle pointed to a hill on the eastern skyline. It was not yet midday, but Hare was up on top of that hill in one flash, looking down eagerly on the other side. There was no sign of a palace anywhere, where the moon might live. He could see nothing but plains rolling up to the farther skyline. He sat down to wait, getting up every few minutes to take another look round. He certainly was excited.

At last the sky grew dark and a few stars lit up. Hare began to strut about so that the moon should see what a fine figure of a creature was waiting for her. He looked first down one side of the hill, then down the other. But she was still nowhere in sight.

Suddenly he saw her – but not coming up his hill. No. There was a black hill on the skyline, much farther to the east, and she was just peeping silver over the top of that.

"Ah!" cried Hare. "I've been waiting on the wrong hill. I'll miss her if I don't hurry."

He set off towards her at a run. How he ran. Down into the dark valley, and up the hill to the top. But what a surprise he got there! The moon had gone. Ahead of him, across another valley, was another skyline, another black hill – and that was the hill the moon was climbing.

"Wait for me! Wait!" Hare cried, and set off again down into the valley.

That night Hare was out early, but it was just the same. Again he found himself waiting on the wrong hill. The moon came over the black crest of a hill on the skyline far to the east of him. Hill by hill, he chased her into the east over four hills, but at last she was alone in the sky above him. Then, no matter how he leapt and called after her, she went sailing on up the sky. So he sat and listened and listened to hear what she was saying about him. He could hear nothing.

"Her voice is so soft," Hare told himself.

He set off in good time for the hill in the west where she had gone down the night before, but again he seemed to have misjudged it. She came down on the hilly skyline that was farther again to the west of him, and again he was too late.

Oh, how he longed to marry the moon. Night after night he waited for her, but never once could he hit on the right hill.

Poor Hare! He didn't know that when the moon seemed to be rising from the nearest hill in the east or falling on to the nearest hill in the west, she was really rising and falling over the far, far edge of the world, beyond all hills. Such a trick the creatures had played on him, saying the moon wanted to marry him.

But he didn't give up.

Soon he began to change. With endlessly gazing at the moon, he began to get the moonlight in his eyes, giving him a wild, startled look. And with racing from hill to hill he grew to be a wonderful runner. Especially up the hills – he just shot up them. And from leaping to reach her when he was too late, he came to be a great leaper. And from listening and listening, all through the night, for what the moon was saying high in the sky, he got his long, long ears.

Ted Hughes

"THE WHITE OWL"

from LOVE IN THE VALLEY

Lovely are the curves of the white owl sweeping
Wavy in the dusk lit by one large star.
Lone on the fir-branch, his rattle-note unvaried,
Brooding o'er the gloom, spins the brown eve-jar.

George Meredith

FLYING CROOKED

The butterfly, a cabbage-white,
(His honest idiocy of flight)
Will never now, it is too late,
Master the art of flying straight,
Yet has – who knows so well as I? –
A just sense of how not to fly:
He lurches here and here by guess
And God and hope and hopelessness.
Even the aerobatic swift
Has not his flying-crooked gift.

Robert Graves

from WILD ANIMALS I HAVE KNOWN

In his books, Ernest Thompson Seton emphasises our kinship with the animal world, by showing that in animals we can find the virtues most admired in Man, such as the wolf's dignity during captivity.

We tied his feet securely, but he never groaned, nor growled, nor turned his head. Then with our united strength were just able to put him on my horse. His breath came evenly as though sleeping, and his eyes were bright and clear again, but did not rest on us. Afar on the great rolling mesas they were fixed, his passing kingdom, where his famous band was now scattered. And he gazed till the pony descended the pathway into the cañon, and the rocks cut off the view.

By travelling slowly we reached the ranch in safety, and after securing him with a collar and a strong chain, we staked him out in the pasture and removed the cords. Then for the first time I could examine him closely, and proved how unreliable is vulgar report when a living hero or tyrant is concerned. He had *not* a collar of gold about his neck, nor was there on his shoulders an inverted cross to denote that he had leagued himself with Satan. But I did find on one haunch a great broad scar, that tradition says was the fang-mark of Juno, the leader of Tannerey's wolf-hounds – a mark which she gave him the moment before he stretched her lifeless on the sand of the cañon.

I set meat and water beside him, but he paid no heed. He lay calmly on his breast, and gazed with those steadfast yellow eyes away past me down through the gateway of the cañon, over the open plains – his plains – nor moved a muscle when I touched him. When the sun went down he was still gazing fixedly across the prairie. I expected he would call up his band when night came, and prepared for them, but he had called once in his extremity, and none had come; he would never call again.

A lion shorn of his strength, an eagle robbed of his freedom, or a dove bereft of his mate, all die, it is said, of a broken heart; and who will aver that this grim bandit could bear the three-fold brunt, heart-whole? This only I know, that when the morning dawned, he was lying there still in his position of calm repose, his body unwounded, but his spirit was gone – the old King-wolf was dead.

Ernest Thompson Seton

from BLACK BEAUTY

The first place that I can well remember was a large pleasant meadow with a pond of clear water in it. Some shady trees leaned over it, and rushes and water-lilies grew at the deep end. Over the hedge on one side we looked into a ploughed field, and on the other we looked over a gate at our master's house, which stood by the roadside; at the top of the meadow was a plantation of fir trees, and at the bottom a running brook overhung by a steep bank.

Whilst I was young I lived upon my mother's milk, as I could not eat grass. In the day time I ran by her side, and at night I lay down close by her. When it was hot, we used to stand by the pond in the shade of the trees, and when it was cold, we had a nice warm shed near the plantation.

As soon as I was old enough to eat grass, my mother used to go out to work in the day time, and came back in the evening.

There were six young colts in the meadow besides me; they were older than I was; some were nearly as large as grown-up horses. I used to run with them, and had great fun; we used to gallop all together round and round the field, as hard as we could go. Sometimes we had rather rough play, for they would frequently bite and kick as well as gallop.

One day, when there was a good deal of kicking, my mother whinnied to me to come to her, and then she said:

"I wish you to pay attention to what I am going to say to you. The colts who live here are very good colts, but they are cart-horse colts, and, of course, they have not learned manners. You have been well bred and well born; your father has a great name in these parts, and your grandfather won the cup two years at the Newmarket races; your grandmother had the sweetest temper of any horse I ever knew, and I think you have never seen me kick or bite. I hope you will grow up gentle and good, and never learn bad ways; do your work with a good will, lift your feet up well when you trot, and never bite or kick even in play."

I have never forgotten my mother's advice; I knew she was a wild old horse, and our master thought a great deal of her. Her name was Duchess, but he often called her Pet.

Our master was a good, kind man. He gave us good food, good lodging, and kind words; he spoke as kindly to us as he did to his little children. We were all fond of him, and my mother loved him very much. When she saw him at the gate, she would neigh with joy, and trot up to him. He would pat and stroke her, and say, "Well, old Pet, and how is your little Darkie?" I was a dull black, so he called me Darkie; then he would give me a piece of bread, which was very good, and sometimes he brought a carrot for my mother. All the horses would come to him, but I think we were his favourites. My mother always took him to the town on a market day in a little gig.

There was a ploughboy, Dick, who sometimes came into our field to pluck blackberries from the hedge. When he had eaten all he wanted, he would have what he called fun with the colts, throwing stones and sticks at them to make them gallop. We did not much mind him, for we could gallop off; but sometimes a stone would hit and hurt us.

One day he was at this game, and did not know that the master was in the next field; but he was there, watching what was going on: over the hedge he jumped in a snap, and catching Dick by the arm, he gave him such a box on the ear as made him roar with the pain and surprise. As soon as we saw the master, we trotted up nearer to see what went on.

"Bad boy!" he said, "bad boy! to chase the colts. This is not the first time, nor the second, but it shall be the last – there – take your money and go home, I shall not want you on my farm again." So we never saw Dick any more. Old Daniel, the man who looked after the horses, was just as gentle as our master, so we were well off.

Anna Sewell

from REYNARD THE FOX

On old Cold Crendon's windy tops
  Grows wintrily Blown Hilcote Copse,
    Wind-bitten beech with badger barrows,
    Where brocks eat wasp-grubs with their marrows,
  And foxes lie on short-grassed turf,
  Nose between paws, to hear the surf
Of wind in the beeches drowsily.
  There was our fox bred lustily
    Three years before, and there he berthed,
    Under the beech-roots snugly earthed,
      With a roof of flint and a floor of chalk
      And ten bitten hens' heads each on its stalk,
        Some rabbits' paws, some fur from scuts,
        A badger's corpse and a smell of guts.
          And there on the night before my tale
          He trotted out for a point in the vale.

        He saw, from the cover edge, the valley
          Go trooping down with its droops of sally
          To the brimming river's lipping bend,
          And a light in the inn at Water's End.
          He heard the owl go hunting by
            And the shriek of the mouse the owl made die,
            And the purr of the owl as he tore the red
            Strings from between his claws and fed;
          The smack of joy of the horny lips
          Marbled green with the blobby strips.

60

He saw the farms where the dogs were barking,
Cold Crendon Court and Copsecote Larking;
The fault with the spring as bright as gleed,
Green-slash-laced with water-weed.
A glare in the sky still marked the town,
Though all folk slept and the blinds were down,
The street lamps watched the empty square,
The night-cat sang his evil there.

The fox's nose tipped up and round,
Since smell is a part of sight and sound.
Delicate smells were drifting by,
The sharp nose flaired them heedfully;
Partridges in the clover stubble,
Crouched in a ring for the stoat to nubble.
Rabbit bucks beginning to box;
A scratching place for the pheasant cocks,
A hare in the dead grass near the drain,
And another smell like the spring again.

A faint rank taint like April coming,
It cocked his ears and his blood went drumming,
For somewhere out by Ghost Heath Stubs
Was a roving vixen wanting cubs.
Over the valley, floating faint
On a warmth of windflaw, came the taint;
He cocked his ears, he upped his brush,
And he went upwind like an April thrush.

John Masefield

from THE PRIVATE LIFE OF THE RABBIT

Rabbits are as full of moods as humans are, or any other advanced species of mammal. They are extremely sensitive to visual impressions. They respond to a display of *joie de vivre* in a neighbour who jumps into the air of a fine afternoon, for they will do the same.

In man, family 'togetherness' is also important, and it is tolerated by the father rabbit in much the same degree. Provided the young ones are docile they are welcome to stay at home and be treated affectionately as subordinate beings.

Rabbits are so human. Or is it the other way round – humans are so rabbit?

R. M. Lockley

from WATERSHIP DOWN

Escaping the threat to their home, the rabbits of Watership Down are faced with the dangers of crossing a river. But Fiver is too tired to swim and Pipkin is injured.

Hazel felt at a loss. In front of him stood Bigwig, sodden wet, undaunted, single-minded – the very picture of decision. At his shoulder was Fiver, silent and twitching. He saw Blackberry watching him intently, waiting for his lead and disregarding Bigwig's. Then he looked at Pipkin, huddled into a fold of sand, more panic-stricken and helpless than any rabbit he had ever seen. At this moment, up in the wood, there broke out an excited yelping and a jay began to scold.

Hazel spoke through a kind of light-headed trance. "Well, you'd better get on, then," he said, "and anyone else who wants to. Personally, I'm going to wait until Fiver and Pipkin are fit to tackle it."

During the last few minutes Hazel had been as near to losing his head as he was ever to come. He had been at his wits' end, with no reply to Bigwig's scornful impatience except his readiness to risk his own life in company with Fiver and Pipkin. He still could not understand what had happened, but at least he realized that Blackberry wanted him to show authority. His head cleared.

"Swim," he said. "Everybody swim."

He watched them as they went in. Dandelion swam as well as he ran, swiftly and easily. Silver, too, was strong. The others paddled and scrambled over somehow and as they began to reach the other side, Hazel plunged. The cold water penetrated his fur almost at once. His breath came short and as his head went under he could hear a faint grating of gravel along the bottom. He paddled across awkwardly, his head tilted high out of the water, and made for the figwort. As he pulled himself out, he looked round among the sopping rabbits in the alders.

"Where's Bigwig?" he asked.

"Behind you," answered Blackberry, his teeth chattering.

Bigwig was still in the water, on the other side of the pool. He had swum to the raft, put his head against it and was pushing it forward with heavy thrusts of his back legs. "Keep still," Hazel heard him say in a quick, gulping voice. Then he sank. But a moment later he was up again and had thrust his head over the back of the board. As he kicked and struggled, it tilted and then, while the rabbits watched from the bank, moved slowly across the pool and grounded on the opposite side. Fiver pushed Pipkin on to the stones and Bigwig waded out beside them, shivering and breathless.

"I got the idea once Blackberry had shown us," he said. "But it's hard to push it when you're in the water. I hope it's not long to sunrise. I'm cold. Let's get on."

There was no sign of the dog as they made haste through the alders and up the field to the first hedgerow. Most of them had not understood Blackberry's discovery of the raft and at once forgot it. Fiver, however, came over to where Blackberry was lying against the stem of a blackthorn in the hedge.

"You saved Pipkin and me, didn't you?" he said. "I don't think Pipkin's got any idea what really happened; but I have."

"I admit it was a good idea," replied Blackberry. "Let's remember it. It might come in handy again some time."

Richard Adams

from THE SHELL COUNTRY BOOK

A badger sett may be very extensive, a vast labyrinth of tunnels and chambers with many entrances scattered over a wide area, or it may be quite small with one or two entrances only. Much depends upon the type of soil and the ease of digging.

Setts are most usually found in woods or copses, especially where these are bounded by pasture, but you may come across them in hedgerows or in quarries, on sea cliffs, on open moorland and even on rocky mountain sides. At the mouth of each entrance is a large pile of earth, in which vegetation such as bracken, leaves, hay or moss is incorporated. This is the old bedding which has been discharged with the soil when the badgers have been digging. The tunnels are at least twice the diameter of a rabbit's, though the actual entrance may be much bigger than this, owing to continual usage.

Proof that it is a badger sett can usually be obtained by breaking up some of the lumps of earth from the heap outside the entrance; badger hairs can easily be discovered in this way. The hairs are straight and wiry, and are light at the two ends with a darker band between, nearer to the tip.

You can sometimes find badger hairs caught in the lowest strand of barbed wire round the edge of a wood where an obvious animal run comes out into the field. By following these paths back into the wood it will not be long before you find the sett.

For watching I much prefer a sett with only a few entrances. Your chances of seeing a badger are then so much greater. It is wise to make sure beforehand if the sett is occupied, since badgers move from one sett to another periodically. There are various indications of present occupation. Fresh bedding dropped near the entrance is a good sign; also the presence of flies going in and out of the entrance. Fresh dung in shallow pits near the sett is useful confirmation. A cobweb over the entrance usually indicates that the badgers are not at home.

To make quite sure which holes should be watched, place a stick vertically across each one the night before. A badger is sure to knock it over.

Geoffrey Grigson

Soon Lurvy appeared with slops for breakfast. Wilbur rushed out, ate everything in a hurry, and licked the trough. The sheep moved off down the lane, the gander waddled along behind them, pulling grass. And then, just as Wilbur was settling down for his morning nap, he heard again the thin voice that had addressed him the night before.

"Salutations!" said the voice.

Wilbur jumped to his feet. "Salu-*what*?" he cried.

"Salutations!" repeated the voice.

"What are *they*, and where are *you*?" screamed Wilbur. "Please, *please*, tell me where you are. And what are salutations?"

"Salutations are greetings," said the voice. "When I say 'salutations', it's just my fancy way of saying hello or good morning. Actually, it's a silly expression, and I am surprised that I used it at all. As for my whereabouts, that's easy. Look up here in the corner of the doorway! Here I am. Look, I'm waving!"

At last Wilbur saw the creature that had spoken to him in such a kindly way. Stretched across the upper part of the doorway was a big spider's web, and hanging from the top of the web, head down, was a

large grey spider. She was about the size of a gum-drop. She had eight legs, and she was waving one of them at Wilbur in friendly greeting. "See me now?" she asked.

"Oh, yes indeed," said Wilbur. "Yes indeed! How are you? Good morning! Salutations! Very pleased to meet you. What is your name, please? May I have your name?"

"My name," said the spider, "is Charlotte."

"Charlotte what?" asked Wilbur, eagerly.

"Charlotte A. Cavatica. But just call me Charlotte."

"I think you're beautiful," said Wilbur.

"Well, I *am* pretty," replied Charlotte. "There's no denying that. Almost all spiders are rather nice-looking. I'm not as flashy as some, but I'll do. I wish I could see you, Wilbur, as clearly as you can see me."

"Why can't you?" asked the pig. "I'm right here."

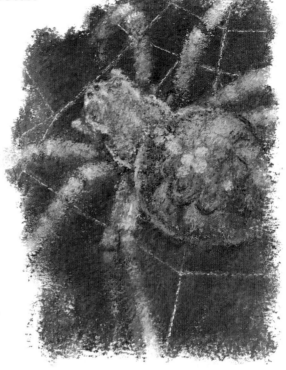

"Yes, but I'm near-sighted," replied Charlotte. "I've always been dreadfully near-sighted. It's good in some ways, not so good in others. Watch me wrap up this fly."

A fly that had been crawling along Wilbur's trough had flown up and blundered into the lower part of Charlotte's web and was tangled in the sticky threads. The fly was beating its wings furiously, trying to break loose and free itself.

"First," said Charlotte, "I dive at him." She plunged headfirst towards the fly. As she dropped, a tiny silken thread unwound from her rear end.

"Next, I wrap him up." She grabbed the fly, threw a few jets of silk round it, and rolled it over and over, wrapping it so that it couldn't move. Wilbur watched in horror. He could hardly believe what he was seeing, and although he detested flies, he was sorry for this one.

"There!" said Charlotte. "Now I knock him out, so he'll be more comfortable." She bit the fly. "He can't feel a thing now," she remarked. "He'll make a perfect breakfast for me."

"You mean you *eat* flies?" gasped Wilbur.

"Certainly. Flies, bugs, grasshoppers, choice beetles, moths, butterflies, tasty cockroaches, gnats, midges, daddy-long-legs, centipedes, mosquitoes, crickets – anything that is careless enough to get caught in my web. I have to live, don't I?"

"Why, yes, of course," said Wilbur. "Do they taste good?"

"Delicious. Of course, I don't really eat them. I drink them – drink their blood. I love blood," said Charlotte, and her pleasant, thin voice grew even thinner and more pleasant.

"Don't say that!" groaned Wilbur. "Please don't say things like that!"

"Why not? It's true, and I have to say what is true. I am not entirely happy about my diet of flies and bugs, but it's the way I'm made. A spider has to pick up a living somehow or other, and I happen to be a trapper. I just naturally build a web and trap flies and other insects. My mother was a trapper before me. Her mother was a trapper before her. All our family have been trappers. Way back for thousands and thousands of years we spiders have been laying for flies and bugs."

"It's a miserable inheritance," said Wilbur, gloomily. He was sad because his new friend was so bloodthirsty.

"Yes, it is," agreed Charlotte. "But I can't help it. I don't know how the first spider in the early days of the world happened to think up this fancy idea of spinning a web, but she did, and it was clever of her, too. And since then, all of us spiders have had to work the same trick. It's not a bad pitch, on the whole."

"It's cruel," replied Wilbur, who did not intend to be argued out of his position.

"Well, *you* can't talk," said Charlotte. "*You* have your meals brought to you in a pail. Nobody feeds me. I have to get my own living. I live by my wits. I have to be sharp and clever, lest I go hungry. I have to think things out, catch what I can, take what comes. And it just so happens, my friend, that what comes is flies and insects and bugs. And *furthermore*," said Charlotte, shaking one of her legs, "do you realize that if I didn't catch bugs and eat them, bugs would increase and multiply and get so numerous that they'd destroy the earth, wipe out everything?"

"Really?" said Wilbur. "I wouldn't want *that* to happen. Perhaps your web is a good thing after all."

E. B. White

THE WILD SWANS AT COOLE

The trees are in their autumn beauty,
The woodland paths are dry,
Under the October twilight the water
Mirrors a still sky;
Upon the brimming water among the stones
Are nine and fifty swans.

The nineteenth Autumn has come upon me
Since I first made my count;
I saw, before I had well finished,
All suddenly mount
And scatter, wheeling, in great broken rings
Upon their clamorous wings.

I have looked upon those brilliant creatures,
And now my heart is sore.
All's changed since I, hearing at twilight,
The first time on this shore,
The bell-beat of their wings above my head,
Trod with a lighter tread.

Unwearied still, lover by lover,
They paddle in the cold,
Companionable streams or climb the air;
Their hearts have not grown old;
Passion or conquest, wander where they will,
Attend upon them still.

But now they drift on the still water
Mysterious, beautiful;
Among what rushes will they build,
By what lake's edge or pool
Delight men's eyes, when I awake some day
To find they have flown away?

William Butler Yeats

from THE NATURAL HISTORY OF SELBORNE

In June last I procured a litter of four or five young hedge-hogs, which appeared to be about five or six days old; they, I find, like puppies, are born blind, and could not see when they came to my hands. No doubt their spines are soft and flexible at the time of their birth, or else the poor dam would have but a bad time of it in the critical moment of parturition: but it is plain that they soon harden; for these little pigs had such stiff prickles on their backs and sides as would easily have fetched blood, had they not been handled with caution. Their spines are quite white at this age; and they have little hanging ears, which I do not remember to be discernible in the old ones. They can, in part, at this age draw their skin down over their faces; but are not able to contract themselves into a ball as they do, for the sake of defence, when full grown. The reason, I suppose, is, because the curious muscle that enables the creature to roll itself up into a ball was not then arrived at its full tone and firmness.

Gilbert White

from WILDLIFE THROUGH THE CAMERA

On mild damp nights earthworms are especially delectable for badgers, as for foxes, and form a large part of their diet particularly in autumn when they spend most of their time feeding in readiness for the rigours of winter. One badger was seen to eat 1,083 worms – that is about one-third of its own bodyweight – in just 90 minutes, each worm neatly plucked from the earth like an elastic strand of freshly cooked spaghetti. In areas where worms are not plentiful, acorns and berries are an alternative diet. Before each night is out the badgers may pay visits to the latrines that border their territory and mark them with the strong secretion that tells badgers from other territories to keep out.

BBC Natural History Unit
Wildlife on One

THE HAIRY DOG

My dog's so furry I've not seen
His face for years and years:
His eyes are buried out of sight,
I only guess his ears.

When people ask me for his breed,
I do not know or care:
He has the beauty of them all
Hidden beneath his hair.

Herbert Asquith

COUNTRY WAYS

Let the mighty and great
Roll in splendour and state,
I envy them not, I declare it.
I eat my own lamb,
My own chicken and ham;
I shear my own sheep and I wear it.

I have lawns and green bowers,
Fresh fruits and fine flowers,
The lark is my bright morning charmer.
So God bless the plough
In the future as now –
Good health and long life to the farmer.

I do not know how she knew, but she must have been wise in the ways of those wise birds, for the next morning she was proven right. She said, "Come down to the pond. You will see for yourself. They have found one of the rooks guilty and turned him out of the rookery."

I followed her down to the pond. I saw that the rookery had ceased to trouble itself with the wicked one. Soon I saw the wicked one himself. He was sitting in a sapling at the edge of the pond, looking very sick indeed.

His feathers were (as it seemed) faded, dirty and staring. His look was that of one sick and without hope.

He did not heed our presence near him: he had been cast out by his community, and our community was a poor thing in comparison with his. We were a poor wingless set who could not lift into the air nor poise on an upper branch fifty or eighty feet in blowing wind. He made no attempt to avoid us. He had been cast out of his community, and that was the end for him.

He did not seem defiant at all: he seemed to feel his situation acutely and to ask for death.

The woman who brought me to see him said that he had committed some crime against rook law, that he was judged for having done this thing, this sin, against rook law. I was not quite sure about this myself. To me he looked very ill indeed and possibly a danger to his community. None of his community had had any mercy for him, and to me he seemed to need mercy, and I would have asked for mercy for him had I known to whom to appeal, and how. He died during the day, and was given a more or less Christian burial under the yew trees.

John Masefield

from LARK RISE TO CANDLEFORD

Old Sally's was a long, low, thatched cottage with diamond-paned windows winking under the eaves and a rustic porch smothered in honeysuckle. Excepting the inn, it was the largest house in the hamlet, and of the two downstair rooms one was used as a kind of kitchen-storeroom, with pots and pans and a big red crockery water vessel at one end, and potatoes in sacks and peas and beans spread out to dry at the other. The apple crop was stored on racks suspended beneath the ceiling and bunches of herbs dangled below. In one corner stood the big brewing copper in which Sally still brewed with good malt and hops once a quarter. The scent of the last brewing hung over the place till the next and mingled with apple and onion and dried thyme and sage smells, with a dash of soapsuds thrown in, to compound the aroma which remained in the children's memories for life and caused a whiff of any two of the component parts in any part of the world to be recognized with an appreciative sniff and a mental ejaculation of "Old Sally's!"

The inner room – "the house", as it was called – was a perfect snuggery, with walls two feet thick and outside shutters to close at night and a padding of rag rugs, red curtains and feather cushions within. There was a good oak, gate-legged table, a dresser with pewter and willow-pattern plates, and a grandfather's clock that not only told the time, but the day of the week as well. It had even once told the changes of the moon; but the works belonging to that part had stopped and only the fat, full face, painted with eyes, nose and mouth, looked out from the square where the four quarters should have rotated. The clock portion kept such good time that half the hamlet set its own clocks by it. The other half preferred to follow the hooter at the brewery in the market town, which could be heard when the wind was in the right quarter. So there were two times in the hamlet and people would say when asking the hour, "Is that hooter time, or Old Sally's?"

Flora Thompson

IF IT'S EVER SPRING AGAIN

If it's ever spring again,
    Spring again,
I shall go where went I when
Down the moor-cock splashed, and hen,
Seeing me not, amid their flounder,
Standing with my arm around her;
If it's ever spring again,
    Spring again,
I shall go where went I then.

If it's ever summer-time,
    Summer-time,
With the hay crop at the prime,
And the cuckoos – two – in rhyme,
As they used to be, or seemed to,
We shall do as long we've dreamed to,
If it's ever summer-time,
    Summer-time,
With the hay, and bees achime.

Thomas Hardy

from HOUSEHOLD TALES WITH OTHER TRADITIONAL REMAINS

If a girl walk backwards to a pear tree on Christmas Eve, and walk round it three times, she will see the spirit or image of the man who is to be her husband.

On Halloween people go out in the dark and pluck cabbage-stalks. If on this eve you scatter seeds or ashes down a lane, and a girl follows you in the direction in which you have gone, she will be your wife.

If you eat an apple at midnight upon All Halloween, and, without looking behind you, gaze into a mirror, you will see the face of your future husband or wife.

At a wedding let the bride pass small pieces of bride-cake through her wedding-ring, and give them to unmarried men and girls. If they put the pieces under their pillows for three nights, on the third night they will dream of their true lovers.

On New Year's Eve three unmarried girls may adopt the following plan in order to see the spirits of their future husbands. Let them go into a room which has two doors, and set the table with knives, forks, and plates for three guests, and let them wait in the room till twelve o'clock at midnight, at which hour exactly the spirits of their future husbands will come in at one door and go out at the other.

Let a girl take the stone out of a plum, throw the stone in the fire, and say these lines:

If he loves me crack and fly,
If he hates me burn and die.

Then let her mention the name of her sweetheart. If he loves her the stone will crack and fly out of the fire. If he does not love her it will quietly burn to ashes.

On Midsummer Eve let a girl take a sprig of myrtle and lay it in her Prayer Book upon the words of the marriage service, "Wilt thou have this man to be thy wedded husband?" Then let her close the book, put it under her pillow, and sleep upon it. If her lover will marry her the myrtle will be gone in the morning, but if it remains in the book he will not marry her.

On Hallows Eve let a girl cross her shoes upon her bedroom floor in the shape of a T and say these lines:

I cross my shoes in the shape of a T,
Hoping this night my true love to see,
Not in his best or worst array,
But in the clothes of every day.

Then let her get into bed backwards without speaking any more that night, when she will see her future husband in her dreams.

S. O. Addy

from A SHROPSHIRE LAD

Loveliest of trees, the cherry now
Is hung with bloom along the bough,
And stands about the woodland ride
Wearing white for Eastertide.

Now, of my threescore years and ten,
Twenty will not come again,
And take from seventy springs a score,
It only leaves me fifty more.

And since to look at things in bloom
Fifty springs are little room,
About the woodlands I will go
To see the cherry hung with snow.

A. E. Housman

TREES

The Oak is called the King of Trees,
The Aspen quivers in the breeze,
The Poplar grows up straight and tall,
The Pear tree spreads along the wall,
The Sycamore gives pleasant shade,
The Willow droops in watery glade,
The Fir tree useful timber gives,
The Beech amid the forest lives.

Sara Coleridge

from HOME AT GRASMERE

April 15th, Thursday. It was a threatening, misty morning, but mild. We set off after dinner from Eusemere. Mrs Clarkson went a short way with us, but turned back. The wind was furious and we thought we must have returned. We first rested in the large boat-house, then under a furze bush opposite Mr Clarkson's. Saw the plough going into the field. The wind seized our breath. The Lake was rough. There was a boat by itself floating in the middle of the bay below Water Millock. We rested again in the Water Millock Lane. The hawthorns are black and green, the birches here and there greenish, but there is yet more of purple to be seen on the twigs. We got over into a field to avoid some cows – people working. A few primroses by the roadside – woodsorrel flower, the anemone, scentless violets, strawberries, and that starry, yellow flower which Mrs C. calls pile wort. When we were in the woods beyond Gowbarrow Park we saw a few daffodils close to the water-side. We fancied that the lake had floated the seeds ashore, and that the little colony had so sprung up. But as we went along there were more and yet more; and at last, under the boughs of the trees, we saw that there was a long belt of them along the shore, about the breadth of a country turnpike road. I never saw daffodils so beautiful. They grew among the mossy stones about and about them; some rested their heads upon these stones as on a pillow for weariness; and the rest tossed and reeled and danced, and seemed as if they verily laughed with the wind, that blew upon them over the lake; they looked so gay, ever glancing, ever changing. This wind blew directly over the lake to them. There was here and there a little knot, and a few stragglers a few yards higher up; but they were so few as not to disturb the simplicity, unity, and life of that one busy highway.

Dorothy Wordsworth

THE LEANING WILLOW

The spinney is long and narrow, threaded by a small stream. Its trees are mainly spindly ash, with some sycamore, hazel, holly and elder. By the stream are alder and a few old willow trees.

The undergrowth is a thick tangle of brier and bramble and giant nettles. Only at the eastern end, where the spinney meets the lane, are there trees of any virtue. Here stands on parade a well dressed rank of seven fine horse-chestnuts, their right hand marker a single beech.

Halfway along the southern fringe is a crab, whose little apples shone brightly in the autumn sunshine as we walked beneath it one late September morning.

Then we saw the fox.

He slipped into the far end of the spinney – a dog fox, by the size of him – but when we entered by the same gap, there was no sign of him, and though the three dachshunds marked his line eagerly, they lost scent and interest a little way in.

This scene was re-played on several walks, and always the dachshunds were at fault at the same place, beneath a big old crack-willow. As such trees often do, it leaned out over the stream, its thick trunk at an angle of 45 degrees to the ground.

We never found an earth in the spinney, so always presumed that the dog fox, on hearing or winding us, simply slid out on the far side and away. Till one day as we stood beneath the willow, we chanced to look upwards. There he sat in a comfortable crotch fifteen feet up, paws together, brush curled neatly round him, ears pricked, looking down on us. What a patronising look it was. We left, feeling small.

Dick King-Smith

GOOD-BYE AND KEEP COLD

This saying good-bye on the edge of the dark
And the cold to an orchard so young in the bark
Reminds me of all that can happen to harm
An orchard away at the end of the farm
All winter, cut off by a hill from the house.
I don't want it girdled by rabbit and mouse,
I don't want it dreamily nibbled for browse
By deer, and I don't want it budded by grouse.
(If certain it wouldn't be idle to call
I'd summon grouse, rabbit, and deer to the wall
And warn them away with a stick for a gun.)
I don't want it stirred by the heat of the sun.
(We made it secure against being, I hope,
By setting it out on a northerly slope.)
No orchard's the worse for the wintriest storm.
But one thing about it, it mustn't get warm.
How often already you've had to be told,
"Keep cold, young orchard. Good-bye and keep cold.
Dread fifty above more than fifty below."
I have to be gone for a season or so.
My business awhile is with different trees,
Less carefully nurtured, less fruitful than these,
And such as is done to their wood with an axe –
Maples and birches and tamaracks.

I wish I could promise to lie in the night
And think of an orchard's arboreal plight
When slowly (and nobody comes with a light)
Its heart sinks lower under the sod.
But something has to be left to God.

Robert Frost

from ALONG THE COTSWOLD WAYS

Sheep do not conveniently grow wool of consistent quality all over their bodies, so the first matter is breaking the fleeces and separating the long strands from the short, the coarse from the fine. Scouring is then necessary to remove the natural grease (in medieval times boiling in stale urine was found effective), and the wool has then to be dried – in the open air or in specially warmed and ventilated drying sheds. Dyeing followed if multi-coloured cloth was required, though until well into the eighteenth century undyed cloth and cloth dyed 'in the piece' provided by far the greater part of Cotswold's production. Carding to disentangle the strands by means of spikes set into cards then followed. The wool was then spun into thread or yarn, initially by spindle and distaff, and from early medieval times on simple hand-operated spinning wheels. The thread had to be wound in 'chains', recognised lengths for easy handling. Weaving followed, but except with very fine thread produced a mesh too open for use as cloth. To make the cloth compact, to cause its fibres to 'felt', was the purpose of fulling. This originally meant treading or 'walking' the cloth after it had been soaped or treated with clayey fullers' earth to speed the felting. By early medieval times fulling mills had been built, in which a series of fulling stocks – gigantic wooden hammers each weighing over a hundredweight and powered by a water-driven shaft – rose and fell alternately on to the cloth in the 'stock pit' below; twelve hours' fulling was required to turn new-woven fabric into the famous Cotswold broadcloth. The cloth had then to be dried and after dyeing – a very skilled process – dried again. Then the nap had to be raised by means of teasels, the spiky heads of a specially-grown, large thistle. The 'fluffiness' resulting had to be sheared off – the shears used were long and heavy, and required expert handling – to leave the cloth, after rolling, smooth and ready for market.

G. R. Crosher

Stanton Drew

First you dismantle the landscape.
Take away everything you first
Thought of. Trees must go,
Roads, of course, the church,
Houses, hedges, livestock, a wire
Fence. The river can stay,
But loses its stubby fringe
Of willows. What do you
See now? Grass, the circling
Mendip rim, with its notches
Fresh, like carving. A sky
Like ours, but empty along
Its lower levels. And earth
Stripped of its future, tilted
Into meaning by these stones,
Pitted and unemphatic. Re-create them.
They are the most permanent
Presences here, but cattle, weather,
Archaeologists have rubbed against them.
Still in season they will
Hold the winter sun poised
Over Maes Knoll's white cheek,
Chain the moon's footsteps to
The pattern of their dance.
Stand inside the circle. Put
Your hand on stone. Listen
To the past's long pulse.

U. A. Fanthorpe

from KING HENRY V

For so work the honey-bees,
Creatures that by a rule in nature teach
The act of order to a peopled kingdom.
They have a king, and officers of sorts,
Where some like magistrates correct at home,
Others, like merchants, venture trade abroad,
Others, like soldiers, armed in their stings,
Make boot upon the summer's velvet buds;
Which pillage they with merry march bring home
To the tent-royal of their emperor;
Who, busied in his majesty, surveys
The singing masons building roofs of gold;
The civil citizens kneading up the honey;
The poor mechanic porters crowding in
Their heavy burdens at his narrow gate;
The sad-eyed justice, with his surly hum,
Delivering o'er to executors pale
The lazy yawning drone.

William Shakespeare

A SHEEP FAIR

The day arrives of the autumn fair,
    And torrents fall,
Though sheep in throngs are gathered there,
    Ten thousand all,
Sodden, with hurdles round them reared:
And, lot by lot, the pens are cleared,
And the auctioneer wrings out his beard,
And wipes his book, bedrenched and smeared,
And rakes the rain from his face with the edge of his hand,
    As torrents fall.

The wool of the ewes is like a sponge
    With the daylong rain:
Jammed tight, to turn, or lie, or lunge,
    They strive in vain.
Their horns are soft as finger-nails,
Their shepherds reek against the rails,
The tied dogs soak with tucked-in tails,
The buyers' hat-brims fill like pails,
Which spill small cascades when they shift their stand
    In the daylong rain.

POSTSCRIPT

Time has trailed lengthily since met
 At Pummery Fair
Those panting thousands in their wet
 And woolly wear:
 And every flock long since has bled,
 And all the dripping buyers have sped,
 And the hoarse auctioneer is dead,
 Who "Going – going!" so often said,
As he consigned to doom each meek, mewed band
 At Pummery Fair.

Thomas Hardy

WILTSHIRE DOWNS

The cuckoo's double note
Loosened like bubbles from a drowning throat
Floats through the air
In mockery of pipit, lark and stare.

The stable-boys thud by
Their horses slinging divots at the sky
And with bright hooves
Printing the sodden turf with lucky grooves.

As still as a windhover
A shepherd in his flapping coat leans over
His tall sheep-crook
And shearlings, tegs and yoes cons like a book.

And one tree-crowned long barrow
Stretched like a sow that has brought forth her farrow
Hides a king's bones
Lying like broken sticks among the stones.

Andrew Young

'UP ON THE DOWNS'

Up on the downs the red-eyed kestrels hover,
Eyeing the grass.
The field-mouse flits like a shadow into cover
As their shadows pass.

Men are burning the gorse on the down's shoulder;
A drift of smoke
Glitters with fire and hangs, and the skies smoulder,
And the lungs choke.

Once the tribe did thus on the downs, on these downs burning
Men in the frame,
Crying to the gods of the downs till their brains were turning
And the gods came.

And to-day on the downs, in the wind, the hawks, the grasses,
In blood and air,
Something passes me and cries as it passes,
On the chalk downland bare.

John Masefield

from JOCK OF THE BUSHVELD

I was lying on my side chewing a grass stem, and Jock lay down in front of me a couple of feet away. It was a habit of his: he liked to watch my face, and often when I rolled over to ease one side and lie on the other, he would get up when he found my back turned to him and come round deliberately to the other side and sling himself down in front of me again. There he would lie with his hind legs sprawled on one side, his front legs straight out, and his head resting on his paws. He would lie like that without a move, his little dark eyes fixed on mine. In the loneliness of that evening I looked into his steadfast resolute face with its darker muzzle and bright faithful eyes that looked so soft and brown when there was nothing to do but got so beady black when it came to fighting. I felt very friendly to the comrade who was little more than a puppy still; and he seemed to feel something too; for as I lay there chewing the straw and looking at him, he stirred his stump of a tail in the dust an inch or so from time to time to let me know that he understood all about it and that it was all right as long as we were together.

Sir Percy Fitzpatrick

ARCADIA

When the green woods laugh with the voice of joy,
And the dimpling stream runs laughing by;
When the air does laugh with merry wit,
And the green hill laughs with the noise of it;

When the meadows laugh with lively green,
And the grasshopper laughs in the merry scene;
When Mary, and Susan, and Emily
With their sweet round mouths sing, "Ha, ha, he!"

When the painted birds laugh in the shade,
When our table with cherries and nuts is spread:
Come live, and be merry, and join with me,
To sing the sweet chorus of "Ha, ha, he!"

from THE COUNTRY CHILD

The morning air was sweet with autumn scents, falling elm leaves, bent ferns, bruised wet grass, beech leaves and sycamore. Windfalls, from the great tree that was too old and too tall to climb, dropped with little thuds and lay under Fanny's feet, crunching under her hoofs as she fed on the patch of grass by the gravelled drive.

Everywhere there was a sound of dropping, tiny bumps filled the air, some so soft that only the blackbird heard, the fall of the scarlet fruit from the dark yews, the beech mast littering the woods. The sweet chestnuts bounded on the paths, splitting open and exposing their one sweet kernel and two withered ones. Dan picked them up and ate them, and kicked away the husks. Susan hunted among the leaves and feasted.

Late Glory roses, tea roses with peach-coloured hearts and petals shading to the deepest cream, bloomed on the house, faded, and scattered their brown leaves on the grass beneath. A few chrysanthemums were left, tawny red flowers and little maroon buttons on the green dresses of the bushes.

Sprigs of lad's love lay among the clothes in the oak presses, and the children at school wore bunches of it to keep them healthy now the damp mists were about.

The woods all round the house were heavy with rich-smelling fallen leaves and decaying moss, with scarlet toadstools and enormous fungi which, when Susan kicked them, turned deep purple, the sure sign they were the deadliest of dead poisons, the food of witches.

The robin's note had changed. He twisted the corkscrew in infinitesimal bottles and poured out the sparkling, chuckling winedrops. He became bolder, the little visitor who was always welcome, and stepped with light foot and engaging eye into the shadow of the doorway to see what there was for breakfast. No cats lived at Windystone Hall, to drink the milk and kill the chicks and scare the robins, so he had no one to fear.

Pheasant strolled proudly across the meadows, and carelessly pecked the turnips which lay in the plough fields. They knew they were safe so long as they did not go in the gardens or orchard. Twenty rabbits sat in a hollow of the field, under the crooked crab-apple tree, which leaned its branches down weighted with green crabs. Susan clapped her hands as she stood at the door, to make their white tails bob, but they, too, didn't care.

Alison Uttley

HOME-THOUGHTS, FROM ABROAD

Oh, to be in England
Now that April's there,
And whoever wakes in England
Sees, some morning, unaware,
That the lowest boughs and the brush-wood sheaf
Round the elm-tree bole are in tiny leaf,
While the chaffinch sings on the orchard bough
In England – now!

And after April, when May follows,
And the whitethroat builds, and all the swallows –
Hark! where my blossomed pear-tree in the hedge
Leans to the field and scatters on the clover
Blossoms and dewdrops – at the bent-spray's edge –
That's the wise thrush; he sings each song twice over,
Lest you should think he never could recapture
The first fine careless rapture!
And though the fields look rough with hoary dew,
All will be gay when noontide wakes anew
The buttercups, the little children's dower,
– Far brighter than this gaudy melon-flower!

Robert Browning

AN EVENING SCENE

The sheep-bell tolleth curfew-time;
   The gnats, a busy rout,
Fleck the warm air; the dismal owl
   Shouteth a sleepy shout;
The voiceless bat, more felt than seen,
   Is flitting round about.

The aspen leaflets scarcely stir;
   The river seems to think;
Athwart the dusk, broad primroses
   Look coldly from the brink,
Where, listening to the freshet's noise,
   The quiet cattle drink.

The bees boom past; the white moths rise
   Like spirits from the ground;
The gray flies hum their weary tune,
   A distant, dream-like sound;
And far, far off, to the slumb'rous eve,
   Bayeth an old guard-hound.

Coventry Patmore

from THE LABOURER'S DAILY LIFE

Some of these cottages in summer-time really approach something of that Arcadian beauty which is supposed to prevail in the country. Everything, of course, depends upon the character of the inmates. The dull tint of the thatch is relieved here and there by great patches of sillgreen, which is religiously preserved as a good herb, though the exact ailments for which it is 'good' are often forgotten. One end of the cottage is often completely hidden with ivy, and woodbine grows in thickest profusion over the porch. Near the door there are almost always a few cabbage-rose trees, and under the windows grow wall-flowers and hollyhocks, sweet peas, columbine, and sometimes the graceful lilies of the valley. The garden stretches in a long strip from the door, one mass of green. It is enclosed by thick hedges, over which the dog-rose grows, and the wild convolvulus will blossom in the autumn. Trees fill up every available space and corner – apple trees, pear trees, damsons, plums, bullaces – all varieties. The cottagers seem to like to have at least one tree of every sort. These trees look very nice in the spring when the apple blossom is out, and again in the autumn when the fruit is ripe. Under the trees are gooseberry bushes, raspberries, and numbers of currants. The patches are divided into strips producing potatoes, cabbage, lettuce, onions, radishes, parsnips; in this kitchen produce, as with the fruit, they like to possess a few of all kinds. There is generally a great bunch of rhubarb. In odd corners there are sure to be a few specimens of southernwood, mugwort, and other herbs; not for use, but from adherence to the old customs. The 'old people' thought much of these 'yherbs', so they must have some too, as well as a little mint and similar potherbs. In the windows you may see two or three geraniums, and over the porch a wicker cage, in which the 'ousel cock, with orange-tawny bill', pours out his rich, melodious notes. There is hardly a cottage without its captive bird, or tame rabbit, or mongrel cur, which seems as much attached to his master as more high-bred dogs to their owners.

Richard Jefferies

from CIDER WITH ROSIE

Summer was also the time of these: of sudden plenty, of slow hours and actions, of diamond haze and dust on the eyes, of the valley in post-vernal slumber; of burying birds out of seething corruption; of Mother sleeping heavily at noon; of jazzing wasps and dragonflies, haystooks and thistle-seeds, snows of white butterflies, skylarks' eggs, bee-orchids, and frantic ants; of wolf-cub parades, and boy scouts' bugles; of sweat running down the legs; of boiling potatoes on bramble fires, of flames glass-blue in the sun; of lying naked in the hill-cold stream; begging pennies for bottles of pop; of girls' bare arms and unripe cherries, green apples and liquid walnuts; of fights and falls and new-scabbed knees, sobbing pursuits and flights; of picnics high up in the crumbling quarries, of butter running like oil, of sunstroke, fever, and cucumber peel stuck cool to one's burning brow. All this, and the feeling that it would never end, that such days had come for ever, with the pump drying up and the water-butt crawling, and the chalk ground hard as the moon. All sights twice-brilliant and smells twice-sharp, all game-days twice as long. Double charged as we were, like the meadow ants, with the frenzy of the sun, we used up the light to its last violet drop, and even then couldn't go to bed.

When darkness fell, and the huge moon rose, we stirred to a second life. Then boys went calling along the roads, wild slit-eyed animal calls, Walt Kerry's naked nasal yodel, Boney's jackal scream. As soon as we heard them we crept outdoors, out of our stifling bedrooms, stepped out into moonlight warm as the sun to join our chalk-white, moon-masked gang.

Games in the moon. Games of pursuit and capture. Games that the night demanded. Best of all, Fox and Hounds – go where you like, and the whole of the valley to hunt through. Two chosen boys loped away

through the trees and were immediately swallowed in shadow. We gave them five minutes, then set off after them. They had churchyard, farmyard, barns, quarries, hilltops, and woods to run to. They had all night, and the whole of the moon, and five miles of country to hide in....

Padding softly, we ran under the melting stars, through sharp garlic woods, through blue blazed fields, following the scent by the game's one rule, the question and answer cry. Every so often, panting for breath, we paused to check on our quarry. Bullet heads lifted, teeth shone in the moon. "Whistle-or-'OLLER! Or-we-shall-not-FOLLER!" It was a cry on two notes, prolonged. From the other side of the hill, above white fields of mist, the faint fox-cry came back. We were off again then, through the waking night, among sleepless owls and badgers, while our quarry slipped off into another parish and would not be found for hours.

Round about midnight we ran them to earth, exhausted under a haystack. Until then we had chased them through all the world, through jungles, swamps, and tundras, across pampas plains and steppes of wheat and plateaux of shooting stars, while hares made love in the silver grasses, and the large hot moon climbed over us, raising tides in my head of night and summer that move there even yet.

Laurie Lee

124

SPRING QUIET

Gone were but the Winter,
Come were but the Spring,
I would go to a covert
Where the birds sing.

Where in the whitethorn
Singeth a thrush,
And a robin sings
In the holly-bush.

Full of fresh scents
Are the budding boughs
Arching high over
A cool green house:

Full of sweet scents
And whispering air
Which sayeth softly:
"We spread no snare;

Here dwell in safety,
Here dwell alone,
With a clear stream
And a mossy stone.

Here the sun shineth
Most shadily;
Here is heard an echo
Of the far sea,
Though far off it be."

Christina Rossetti

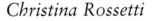

THE CROCUS

The golden crocus reaches up
To catch a sunbeam in her cup.

Walter Crane

from SUMMER IMAGES

I love at early morn from new mown swath
To see the startled frog his rout pursue
And mark while leaping oer the dripping path
   His bright sides scatter dew
And early lark that from its bustle flyes –
   To hail his mattin new
   And watch him to the skyes

And note on hedgerow baulks in moisture sprent
The jetty snail creep from the mossy thorn
In earnest heed and tremolous intent
   Frail brother of the morn
That from the tiney bents and misted leaves
   Withdraws his timid horn
   And fearful vision weaves

And swallows heed on smoke tanned chimney top
As wont be first unsealing mornings eye
Ere yet the bee hath gleaned one wayward drop
   Of honey on his thigh
And see him seek morns airy couch to sing
   Untill the golden sky
   Besprents his russet wing

And sawning boy by tanning corn espy
With clapping noise to startle birds away
And hear him bawl to every passer bye
    To know the hour of day
And see the uncradled breeze refreshed and strong
    With waking blossoms play
    And breath eolian song

I love the south west wind or low or loud
And not the less when sudden drops of rain
Moistens my glowing cheek from ebon cloud
    Threatening soft showers again
That over lands new ploughed and meadow grounds
    Summers sweet breath unchains
    And wakes harmonious sounds

Rich music breaths in summers every sound
And in her harmony of varied greens
Woods meadows hedgrows cornfields all around
    Much beauty intervenes
Filling with harmony the ear and eye
    While oer the mingling scenes
    Far spreads the laughing sky

John Clare

BALLAD OF JOHNNY APPLESEED

Through the Appalachian valleys, with his kit a buckskin bag,
Johnny Appleseed went plodding past high peak and mountain crag.
Oh, his stockings were of leather, and his moccasins were tough;
He was set upon a journey where the going would be rough.

See him coming in the springtime,
Passing violets in the glade.
Many apple trees are needed,
And the pioneers want shade.

Johnny carried many orchards in the bag upon his back,
And the scent of apple blossoms always lingered in his track.
Over half a fertile continent he planted shiny seed;
He would toss them in the clearings where the fawn and yearling feed.

In the summer see him tramping
Through the windings of the wood.
Big red apples in the oven
Make the venison taste good.

He would wander over mountain; he would brave a raging stream,
For his eyes were filled with visions like an ancient prophet's dream.
He would travel after nightfall, start again at early morn;
He was planting seeds of apples for the children yet unborn.

Where the autumn leaves turned crimson,
He was eager to explore.
Apple dumplings never blossomed
On a shady sycamore.

Johnny travelled where the war whoop of the painted tribes rang loud;
And he walked among grim chieftains and their hot-eyed warrior crowd.
He told them of his vision, of his dream that would not die,
So he never was molested, and the settlers had their pie.

Bitter winter found him trudging,
Not for glory or applause,
Only happy for the winesaps
In tomorrow's applesauce!

Helmer O. Oleson

"You must keep still and be quiet," said Mrs Oldknow, laughing at him.

Tolly tried hard to obey her, but their beaks and little wiry clutching hands felt so queer that he had to shut his eyes and screw up his face to keep still. The tits hung on underneath and tickled in unexpected places.

While he was standing there pulling faces he heard a laugh so like a boy's that he could not believe his great-grandmother had made it, and opened his eyes to see who was there. There was no one else. Mrs Oldknow's eyes were fixed on his. The blackbirds were scolding in the branches because they were afraid to come on to his hands and could see that the margarine was nearly finished. Then with a squabbling noise, like a crowd of rude people off a football bus, a flock of starlings arrived, snatching and pushing and behaving badly in every way.

"That will do," said Mrs Oldknow. "Starlings don't wait to be introduced to anybody. I'll give them some bread, and you can wipe your hands on these crusts and throw them to the blackbirds. Then run and wash your hands."

Lucy Boston

from THE LONE SWALLOWS

I was alone with the wheat that I loved. Moving over the field my feet were drenched in an instant by the dew. Lying at full length on the earth, I pressed my face among the sweet wistfulness of stalks, stained and glowing as with some lambent fire, pale, mysterious. On each pale flame-blade depended a small white light, a dew-drop in which the light of the moon was imprisoned. Each flag of wheat held the beauty of pure water, and within the sappy blades glowed the spirit of the earth – in the spectral silence a voice spoke of its ancient lineage: of the slow horses that had strained to the wooden plough through the ages, scarring the glebe in long furrows that must be sown with corn; race after race of slow horses moving in jangling harness to the deep shouts of the heavy men. Generation after generation of men, bent with age and unceasing labour, plodding the earth, sowing the yellow grains that would produce a million million berries for mankind. Spring after spring, each with its glory of blue-winged swallows speeding, wheeling, falling through the azure, the cuckoo calling in the meadows, and the lark-song shaking its silver earthchain as it strove to be free. Through all the sowings and the reapings for thousands of years the wheat had known that it was grown for man, and the soul of the wheat grew in the knowledge of its service. Lying there on the cool couch of the silver-flotten corn, with the soft earth under me, sweet with its scent of stored sunbeams, the beauty of the phantom wheat carried me away in a passion of sweet ecstasy. Faint as the sea-murmur within the shell, the voice of the corn came to the inward ear.

Henry Williamson

from THE WIND IN THE WILLOWS

He thought his happiness was complete when, as he meandered aimlessly along, suddenly he stood by the edge of a full-fed river. Never in his life had he seen a river before – this sleek, sinuous, full-bodied animal, chasing and chuckling, gripping things with a gurgle and leaving them with a laugh, to fling itself on fresh playmates that shook themselves free, and were caught and held again. All was a-shake and a-shiver – glints and gleams and sparkles, rustle and swirl, chatter and bubble. The Mole was bewitched, entranced, fascinated. By the side of the river he trotted as one trots, when very small, by the side of a man, who holds one spellbound by exciting stories; and when tired at last, he sat on the bank, while the river still chattered on to him, a babbling procession of the best stories in the world, sent from the heart of the earth to be told at last to the insatiable sea.

Kenneth Grahame

from TOM'S MIDNIGHT GARDEN

Tom opened the door wide and let in the moonlight. It flooded in, as bright as daylight – the white daylight that comes before the full rising of the sun. The illumination was perfect, but Tom did not at once turn to see what it showed him on the clock-face. Instead he took a step forward on to the doorstep. He was staring, at first in surprise, then with indignation, at what he saw outside. That they should have deceived him – lied to him – like this! They had said, "It's not worth your while going out at the back, Tom." So carelessly they had described it: "A sort of back-yard, very poky, with rubbish bins. Really, there's nothing to see."

Nothing... Only this: a great lawn where flower-beds bloomed; a towering fir-tree, and thick, beetle-browed yews that humped their shapes down two sides of the lawn; on the third side, to the right, a greenhouse almost the size of a real house; from each corner of the lawn, a path that twisted away to some other depths of garden, with other trees.

Tom had stepped forward instinctively, catching his breath in surprise; now he let his breath out in a deep sigh. He would steal out here tomorrow, by daylight. They had tried to keep this from him, but they could not stop him now – not his aunt, nor his uncle, nor the back-flat tenants, nor even particular Mrs Bartholomew. He would run full tilt over the grass, leaping the flower-beds; he would peer through the glittering panes of the greenhouse – perhaps open the door and go in; he would visit each alcove and archway clipped in the yew-trees – he would climb the trees and make his way from one to another through thickly interlacing branches. When they came calling him, he would hide, silent and safe as a bird, among this richness of leaf and bough and tree-trunk.

The scene tempted him even now: it lay so inviting and clear before him – clear-cut from the stubby leaf-pins of the nearer yew-trees to the curled-back petals of the hyacinths in the crescent-shaped corner beds. Yet Tom remembered his ten hours and his honour. Regretfully he turned from the garden, back indoors to read the grandfather clock.

Philippa Pearce

FAREWELL TO THE FARM

The coach is at the door at last;
The eager children, mounting fast
And kissing hands, in chorus sing:
"Good-bye, good-bye, to everything!

"To house and garden, field and lawn,
The meadow-gates we swung upon,
To pump and stable, tree and swing,
Good-bye, good-bye, to everything!

"And fare you well for evermore,
O ladder at the hayloft door,
O hayloft where the cobwebs cling,
Good-bye, good-bye, to everything!"

Crack goes the whip, and off we go;
The trees and houses smaller grow;
Last, round the woody turn we swing:
"Good-bye, good-bye, to everything!"

Robert Louis Stevenson

INDEX OF TITLES AND FIRST LINES

Titles are in *italics*. Where the title and the first line are the same, the first line only is listed.

A

A gypsy, a gypsy   20
A Pig is Never Blamed   65
A pig is never blamed in case   65
A Sheep Fair   110
A Shropshire Lad   100
Akenfield   88
Along the Cotswold Ways   106
An Evening Scene   119
An Introduction to Dogs   62
And the good Nokomis answered   28
August   90

B

Ballad of Johnny Appleseed   128
Being Gypsy   20
Black Beauty   56
"Bread and cheese" grow wild in the
    green time   35

C

Change in the Village   25
Charlotte's Web   76
Cider with Rosie   122
Country Matters   92
Cows   46

F

Farewell to the Farm   138
First you dismantle the landscape   108
Flying Crooked   53
For so work the honey-bees   109

G

Gone were but the Winter   125
Good-bye and Keep Cold   104
Grace Before Ploughing   93

H

Half the time they munched the grass,
    and all the time they lay   46
Hedges   35
Hiawatha's Childhood   28
High, high in the branches   130
Home at Grasmere   101
Home-Thoughts, From Abroad   118
*Household Tales with other Traditional
    Remains*   98
How the Hare Became   48

I

I love at early morn from new mown
    swath   126
I will go with my Father a-ploughing   36
If it's ever spring again   97
In February there are days   130
In winter-time we go   16

J

Jock of the Bushveld   114
Jude the Obscure   29

K

Kilvert's Diary 1870-1879   12
King Henry V   109

L

Lark Rise to Candleford   95

Let the mighty and great   87

Love in the Valley   53

Loveliest of trees, the cherry now   100

Lovely are the curves of the white owl
      sweeping   53

M

Minnows   42

My dog's so furry I've not seen   86

O

Oh, to be in England   118

On old Cold Crendon's windy tops   60

R

Reynard the Fox   60

S

Salar the Salmon   44

Spring Quiet   125

Stanton Drew   108

Still Glides the Stream   24

Summer Images   126

Swarms of minnows show their little
      heads   42

T

Tales of Arabel's Raven   13

Tarka the Otter   73

The butterfly, a cabbage-white   53

The Children of Green Knowe   131

The city dwellers all complain   90

The coach is at the door at last   138

The Country Child   11, 116

The Crocus   125

The Cuckoo   43

The cuckoo is a merry bird   43

The cuckoo's double note   112

The day arrives of the autumn fair   110

The dog is man's best friend   62

The Ferns   130

The golden crocus reaches up   125

The Hairy Dog   86

The Labourer's Daily Life   120

The Leaning Willow   102

The Lone Swallows   21, 133

The Natural History of Selborne   84

The Oak is called the King of Trees   100

The Peppermint Pig   6

The Pig   65

The pig is not a nervous beast   65

The Poacher's Son   17

The Private Life of the Rabbit   66

The robin sings in the elm   37

The Secret Song   72

The sheep-bell tolleth curfew-time   119

The Sheep-Pig   38

The Shell Country Book   74

The Thrush's Nest   64

The trees are in their autumn beauty   82

The View in Winter   27

The Whistler at the Plough   32

The White Owl   53

The Wild Swans at Coole   82

The Wind in the Willows   135

This is the weather the cuckoo likes   91

This saying good-bye on the edge of
      the dark   104

Through the Appalachian valleys, with his kit a buckskin bag 128
Tom's Midnight Garden 136
Trees 100

U

'*Up on the Downs*' 113
Up on the downs the red-eyed kestrels hover 113

W

Watership Down 67
Weathers 91
When 130

When the green woods laugh with the voice of joy 115
Where the pools are bright and deep 5
Whether 90
Whether the weather be fine 90
White Fields 16
Who saw the petals 72
Wild Animals I Have Known 54
Wildlife Through the Camera 85
Wiltshire Downs 112
Within a thick and spreading hawthorn bush 64

Index of Authors

A
Adams, Richard 67
Addy, S. O. 98
Aiken, Joan 13
Aldis, Dorothy 130
Anderson, Rachel 17
Asquith, Herbert 86

B
Baro, Gene 130
Bawden, Nina 6
BBC Natural History Unit 85
Blythe, Ronald 27, 88
Boston, Lucy 131
Bourne, George 25
Brown, Margaret Wise 72
Browning, Robert 118

C
Campbell, Joseph 36
Clare, John 64, 126
Coleridge, Sara 100
Crane, Walter 125
Crosher, G. R. 106

D
Deutsch, Babette 65

F
Fanthorpe, U. A. 108
Fitzpatrick, Sir Percy 114
Frost, Robert 104

G
Grahame, Kenneth 135
Graves, Robert 53
Grigson, Geoffrey 74

Gurney, Ivor 35

H
Hardy, Thomas 29, 91, 97, 110
Housman, A. E. 100
Hughes, Ted 48

J
Jefferies, Richard 120

K
Keats, John 42
Kilvert, The Reverend Francis 12
King-Smith, Dick 38, 102

L
Lee, Laurie 122
Lewis, Michael 90
Lockley, R. M. 66
Longfellow, Henry Wadsworth 28

M
Masefield, John 60, 93, 113
Meredith, George 53

N
Nash, Ogden 62
Niall, Ian 92

O
Oleson, Helmer O. 128

P
Patmore, Coventry 119
Pearce, Philippa 136

R
Reeves, James 46
Rossetti, Christina 125

S
Seton, Ernest Thompson 54
Sewell, Anna 56
Shakespeare, William 109
Somerville, Alexander 32
Stephens, James 16
Stevenson, Robert Louis 138

T
Thompson, Flora 24, 95

U
Uttley, Alison 11, 116

W
White, E. B. 76
White, Gilbert 84
Williamson, Henry 21, 44, 73, 133
Wordsworth, Dorothy 101

Y
Yeats, William Butler 82
Young, Andrew 112
Young, Barbara 20
Young, Roland 65

ACKNOWLEDGEMENTS

The publishers would like to thank the copyright holders for permission to reproduce the following copyright material. Every effort has been made to trace the ownership of all copyrighted material and to secure the necessary permission to reprint these selections. In the event of any question arising as to the use of any material, the editor and publisher, while expressing regret for any inadvertent error, will be happy to make the necessary correction in future printings.

The Peppermint Pig, copyright © Nina Bawden 1975. Reproduced by permission of Curtis Brown, London • *The Country Child*, © Alison Uttley 1931, reproduced by permission of Faber and Faber Ltd • *Tales of Arabel's Raven*, by Joan Aiken (BBC Books, 1974), © Joan Aiken Enterprises Ltd, reproduced by permission of A. M. Heath • 'White Fields' from *Collected Poems* by James Stephens, (Macmillan Publishers), reproduced by permission of The Society of Authors as the Literary Representative of the Estate of James Stephens • *The Poacher's Son*, © Rachel Anderson 1982, reproduced by permission of the author • 'Being Gypsy' from *Christopher O!* by Barbara Young, (David McKay Company, Inc), © Barbara Young, 1947 • *Still Glides the Stream*, by Flora Thompson, (Oxford University Press, 1983), © Flora Thompson, reproduced by permission of Oxford University Press • *Jude the Obscure* by Thomas Hardy, reproduced by permission of Macmillan • 'Hedges' by Ivor Gurney, © Robin Haines, Sole Trustee of the Gurney Estate 1982. Reproduced from *Collected Poems of Ivor Gurney*, edited by P. J. Kavanagh (1982), by permission of Oxford University Press • *Country Matters* by Ian Niall, published by Victor Gollancz, 1984, reproduced by permission of Victor Gollancz • John Masefield: 'The Outcast' from *Grace Before Ploughing: Fragments of an Autobiography*, reproduced by permission of The Society of Authors as the Literary Representative of the Estate of John Masefield • *Lark Rise to Candleford* by Flora Thompson, published by Oxford University Press (1939) • 'Loveliest of trees, the cherry now', from *Collected Poems: A Shropshire Lad* by A. E. Housman, (Jonathan Cape), reproduced by permission of The Society of Authors as the Literary Representative of the Estate of A. E. Housman • 'The Leaning Willow', from *The Tree, A Celebration of Our Living Skyline*; edited by Peter Wood, (David & Charles, 1990), reproduced by permission of Dick King-Smith • 'Good-bye and Keep Cold' by Robert Frost, from *The Poetry of Robert Frost* edited by Edward Connery Lathem, Copyright © 1951 by Robert Frost, copyright 1923, © 1969 by Henry Holt and Company, Inc. Reproduced by permission of Henry Holt and Company, Inc. • 'Stanton Drew' by U. A. Fanthorpe, copyright U. A. Fanthorpe, from *Side Effects* (1978), reproduced by permission of Peterloo Poets • 'Wiltshire Downs' by Andrew Young, from *The Poetical Works of Andrew Young*, edited by Edward Lowbury & Alison Young, (Secker & Warburg, 1985), reproduced by permission of The Andrew Young Estate • 'Up on the Downs' by John Masefield, from *Poems of John Masefield* (Heinemann, 1946), reproduced by permission of The Society of Authors as the Literary Representative of the Estate of John Masefield • *The Sheep-Pig* by Dick King-Smith, (Victor Gollancz/Hamish Hamilton, 1983), copyright © Dick King-Smith, 1983, reproduced by permission of Penguin Books Ltd • *Charlotte's Web* by E. B. White, (Hamish Hamilton Children's Books, 1952) copyright © J White, 1952, reproduced by permission of Frederick Warne & Co • 'How the Hare Became' by Ted Hughes, from *How the Whale Became*, (Faber and Faber), reproduced by permission of Faber and Faber • *Watership Down* by Richard Adams (Rex Collings, 1972, Puffin Books, 1973, Penguin Books, 1974), copyright © Richard Adams, 1972 • 'The Secret Song' by Margaret Wise Brown, from *Nibble, Nibble* by Margaret Wise Brown, published by Addison Wesley Publishing Co, Inc. (1959) • 'The Pig' by Roland Young, from *Not for Children* by Roland Young (Doubleday and Co., Inc., 1930) • 'An Introduction to Dogs' by Ogden Nash, from *I'm a Stranger Here Myself* (Little Brown, 1938), reproduced by permission of Curtis Brown Ltd, copyright © 1938 by Ogden Nash, renewed • 'Cows' by James Reeves, © James Reeves from *Complete Poems for Children* (Heinemann), reproduced by permission of the James Reeves Estate • 'Reynard the Fox Part II' by John Masefield, (Heinemann, 1919), reproduced by permission of The Society of Authors as the Literary Representative of the Estate of John Masefield • *The Shell Country Book* by Geoffrey Grigson (Phoenix House, 1962) • 'The Wild Swans at Coole' by W. B. Yeats, from *The Collected Poems of W. B. Yeats*, (Macmillan, 1950), reproduced by permission of A. P. Watt Ltd on behalf of Michael Yeats • *Wild Animals I Have Known* by Ernest Thompson Seton (Hodder & Stoughton, 1926), © Ernest Thompson Seton, 1926, reproduced by permission of Sheil Land Associates • 'Flying Crooked' by Robert Graves, from *Collected Poems by Robert Graves* (Oxford University Press, 1975), reproduced by permission of Carcanet Press • Extract from *Wildlife Through the Camera*, with the permission of BBC Worldwide Limited • *The Private Life of the Rabbit* by R. M. Lockley (André Deutsch, 1965) • *The Country Child* by Alison Uttley, (Faber and Faber, 1931), reproduced by permission of Faber and Faber Ltd • *Cider with Rosie* by Laurie Lee, (Hogarth Press, 1959) • 'When' by Dorothy Aldis reprinted by permission of G. P. Putnam's Sons from *Hop, Skip and Jump!* by Dorothy Aldis, copyright 1934, © 1961 by Dorothy Aldis • *The Children of Green Knowe* by Lucy Boston (Faber and Faber Ltd, 1954), by permission of Faber and Faber Ltd • *The Wind in the Willows* by Kenneth Grahame, copyright © The University Chest, Oxford, reproduced by permission of Curtis Brown, London • *Tom's Midnight Garden* by Philippa Pearce, (Oxford University Press, 1958), by permission of Oxford University Press • The following poems feature as chapter openers: 'The Boy's Song' by James Hogg, 'The Robin and the Cows' by William Dean Howells, 'The Happy Farmer', an Old English Rhyme' and 'Laughing Song' by William Blake

144